A GHETTO GIRL'S DREAM:
AN AFRICAN-AMERICAN CINDERELLA STORY

A GHETTO GIRL'S DREAM
AN AFRICAN-AMERICAN CINDERELLA STORY

An Inspirational Love Story For My Brothers And Sisters

Written by
Ada Sherrill

Published by
THE SHERRILL GROUP

Copyright 1995 by The Sherrill Group

The Sherrill Group
P.O. Box 6877
Washington, D.C. 20020

Include Scripture quotes
from the King James Version

Library of Congress Cataloging in Publication Data
ISBN 0-9646114-0-6: $20.00 Hard cover

Edited by Alex Lajoux
Cover Photograph Latasha Mills

Printed In The United States of America.

First and far most giving honor to GOD my lord and Savior
and to the Son Jesus Christ for I know that it was you who
made the completion and success of this book possible.
Thank You.

PHILLIPPIANS 4:13   I CAN DO ALL THINGS THROUGH JESUS CHRIST WHICH STRENGTHENS ME.

DEDICATION

This book is dedicated to all the families who have lost their sons, daughters, mothers, fathers, sisters, brothers, husbands, wives, cousins, and friends. I know the feelings you have been through and I know the emptiness that you are left with when someone has brutally murdered a loved one. My dedication and personal condolences to all of you.

I also share this dedication to my husband, mother, sisters, nieces, nephew, and great nephew for the pain of losing my brother T-Bone in December of 1987. Last, but not least to the two people whom I love most in the world and who has helped me make it through the later difficult times of my life, my daughters, Latasha and Ebony.

To my best friend Dorothy Renee' Coates, thank you.

A very special thanks to Gene Collins.

To my brother-in-laws John H. Mills and James T. Harris

ACKNOWLEDGMENTS

To my wonderful mother, Elouise Temoney, I once heard someone say, all that I could ever hope to be and everything that I have become is because of you, this stands true for me too. I love you. Thank you.

To my Darling husband, Bobby Mills, Thank you for supporting me, maintaining patience, and having faith in me. I love you.

To my beautiful daughters, Latasha and Ebony Mills, they are the light that shines on the path that I follow. Thank you for the JOY you bring me. I love you.

To my sisters, Darlene Harris and Kathy Sherrill, Thank You for your support and sharing the times with me. I love you both.

To my best and dear friend, Dorothy Renee' Coates, Some people go through life never being a friend and never having a friend. You have allowed me to share in both. Thank you for being a true friend for more than twenty years and always. I love you.

To Cathy Hughes and the WOL Family members for being my inspiration. Because of you I have Information, Knowledge and Power. You accepted me into your family many years ago and you continue to nourish me daily. Because you share with and inform the community, I can be. Wishing you continued success and I love You. (One of the "C" girls)

Once their lived a man name Job. This man was blameless and upright; he feared GOD and shunned evil. He had seven sons and three daughters. And he owned seven thousand sheep, three thousand camels, five hundred yoke of Exon and five hundred donkeys, and had a large number of servants. He was the greatest man among all the people of the east.

His sons used to take turns holding feasts in their homes, and they would invite their sisters to eat and drink with them. When a period of feasting had run its course, Job would sacrifice burnt offering for each of them, thinking perhaps my children have sinned and cursed GOD in their hearts. This was Job's regular custom.

One day the angels came to present themselves before the lord and Satan also came with them. The Lord said to Satan, "Where have you come from?" Satan answered the Lord, "From roaming through the earth and going back and forth in it."

The Lord said, "Have you considered my servant Job? There is no one on earth like him; he is blameless and upright, a man who fears GOD and shuns evil."

"Does Job fear GOD for nothing?" Satan replied. "Have you not put a hedge around him and his household and everything he has? You have blessed the work of his hands, so that his flocks and herds are spread through the land. But stretch out your hand, and strike everything he has and he will surely curse you to your face."

The Lord said to Satan, "Very well, then , everything he has is in your hands, but on the man himself do not lay a finger."

Then Satan went out from the presence of the Lord.

One day when Job's sons and daughters were feasting and drinking wine at the oldest brother's house, a messenger came to Job and said, "The Oxen were plowing and the donkeys were grazing nearby, and the Sebeans attacked and carried them off. They put the servants to the sword, and I am the only one who has escaped to tell you!"

While he was still speaking, another messenger came and said, "The fire of GOD fell from the sky and burned up the sheep and the servants, and I am the only one who has escaped to tell!"

While he was still speaking, another messenger came and said, "The Chaldeans formed three raiding parties and swept down on you camels and carried them off. They put the servants to the sword, and I am the only one who has escaped to tell you!"

While he was still speaking, yet another messenger came and said, "Your sons and daughters were feasting and drinking wine at the oldest brother's house, when suddenly a mighty wind swept in from the desert and struck the four corners of the house. It collapsed on them and they are dead, and I am the only one who has escaped to tell you!"

At this, Job got up and tore his robe and shaved his head. Then he fell to the ground in worship and said:

"Naked I came from my mother's womb, and naked I will depart.

The Lord gave and the Lord has taken away; may the name of the Lord be praised."

In all this sorrow, Job did not sin by charging GOD with wrongdoing.

JOB 1:1-17

TABLE OF CONTENTS

CHAPTERS

A GIRL NAMED DIANA

The year was 1975, a time when African Americans were getting past making a statement of being black and proud. It was a time when wide-leg pants and the afro's were popular. Colors were in and being in love was like being rich. African Americans had morals and dignity. To respect the next man was cool. Going to a party meant dressing in style. After school on Friday, you would go home and take your best pair of jeans out. The jeans were usually tight-fitted and straight from the top to the bottom. You would get a can of starch and iron the hardest crease down the middle of the jeans. Then you would get a top to match the color of your shoes. At ten o'clock that night a car load of your friends would pick you up and you all would be on your way to the party. When you got there a blue or red light would be on as you walked down the basement steps. In one corner was a food table and next to the food table would be the beer and liquor table. Across the room would be the DJ and his music. You would dance, eat, and rap all night long. And when you left to go home it was daylight outside. The mid-seventies introduced giving peace a chance. Being all you can be was hip and being hip was everything. The life of Diana James had just started to take shape.

Diana was in the tenth grade at Anacostia High School. Anacostia High was a large institution. It was red brick lined with a beige cement brick. The building had a long walkway with three steps spaced apart. The steps led up to the front porch. Inside the walls in the hallways were a dull gray. The front office was made of glass and had windows all around. The classrooms were painted white. The school had three to four hundred students.

Earlier in Diana's life she had gone from being an army brat to a ghetto girl who didn't know what she was going to eat for dinner or if she would eat at all that night.

When Diana was born her mother and father lived on military bases up until she was eight years old. Sheltered from the civilian life, she knew very little about what was going on in the outside world. In the beginning it looked as if Diana would spend the rest of her childhood life with both her parents on military bases. Later Diana would live a completely different life. Diana was born on August 19, 1959 at Walter Reed Army Medical Center in Washington D.C.

Her mother was originally from Weeks Island Louisiana. Weeks Island looked exactly like it sound. It was and island with tall green trees that were divided by gardens. You could see tomatoes, greens, cabbages, corn and sugar cane for miles. The houses were made of wood with brick looking roofing material. The windows were small with stripes of wood going through them. Most of the people on the island were family. The island had horses and cows and chickens. There was a shack near the bayou that looked like it would fall anytime. It was called a Juke Joint. People came from across the bayou to drink liquor and dance all night. After getting drunk they had people who tried to swim back across the bayou and fell to sleep in the water and they slept there all night, faced up Thank God. Diana would look out the window and see them get up and out of the water to go home.

The kids on the island would swim across the bayou to get to the candy store. All the stores were across the bayou. You had to ride a boat across or swim. Diana's grandparent's house was the third house from the water. The two families in front of them were relatives. The island only had about twenty house on it. The grass and trees were green and the sky was so blue. The water was a smooth flowing greenish blue. It was a beautiful place to have lived.

Diana's father was from Memphis, Tennessee. He was the son of a share cropper and the oldest of nine siblings. His father died early in his life and his mother raised them with the help of the oldest children. Diana had never been to Tennessee. Her father wanted to forget his life there and he very seldom talked about it.

In 1961, when she was two years old Diana's father received orders to go to Korea and her mother decided to wait at her parent's house in Louisiana. Diana and her mother lived with her grandparents for two years. While Diana was at her grandfather's house in Louisiana she learned to ride horses, milk a cow, feed the animals, and rise with the sun to the smell of country ham and fried potatoes and eggs, and grits, and fried fat back. Diana's grandfather was a strong black man. He was smart and good looking, women loved to see him coming. They would all be staring with their heads down. Diana's grandmother was pretty, with coal black hair hanging down her back. When Diana's grandmother and mother wanted to keep secrets they spoke in French. Her grandmother was very quiet and made very few decisions. She was very happy standing behind her husband and his words.

Every night Diana would spend time in her grandparent's room learning their way of life. The room had hard wood floors with a shine like glass over it. The bedroom drapes were royal red and the bed spread matched them. The cotton material looked very rich. The sheets and pillow cases were white. They had been ironed with a crease. The two night stands had big shade lamps on them. On Diana's grandmother's side of the bed were cook books and a Bible. Next to her grandfathers side was a Bible and a calendar. The walls had pictures of land and the skies. The house had three bedrooms. All the rooms were the same neat and clean.

Diana learned to be courteous, polite, kind hearted, mannerly, and honest. She was taught to share and give to the needy. Diana was proving to be a very smart young girl. Diana enjoyed learning from her grandparents but she never stopped counting the days away from when it was time for her father to return. Diana's father spent a lot of time reading and teaching her different cultures in different countries. Diana had started to read well by the time she was three. She would never forget what her grandparents taught her and would always reflect on their teachings for the rest of her life.

In 1964 her father came back to the states and was stationed in Hawthorn, California. It was time for Diana to go back to her father. She was excited. Diana liked living in California, she lived only two blocks from the airport and loved seeing the airplanes take off. Her father would take her down the block at night to see the planes and the lit-up run ways. Diana and her mother spent a lot of time shopping and sight-seeing in California while her father was at work. Diana was able to get anything she wanted and her mother was glad to buy it for her. Diana went to visit the area where the stars lived and the blocks in Hollywood where they had stars. Diana had cousins in LA also that she visited a lot.

Diana loved living in LA. When she started kindergarten in there she was far advanced over the other students and the teachers as well as the students loved her. Diana's father would go to work and tell his co-workers about how the school liked to hear Diana talk with her southern accent. And how they loved the way she had so much joy. Diana's father said that even the sad became joyful when Diana was around.

Diana lived in LA with her mother and father for two years before they moved to EL Paso, Texas. Diana was six years old by now and Texas felt some how like familiar grounds. It reminded her of her hometown in Louisiana. She went to school with a lot of kids that were raised in the same manner as she was. A lot of the kids had grandparents like Diana. In Louisiana, family members were important to each other. Diana lived next door to some mexicans name Ranko, who were very friendly. The Ranko's liked

Diana very much. She learned from them and they learned from her. They spent a lot of time over each other's houses. The one thing Diana knew well was how to be a friend and treat people.

By the time Diana was in the second grade her mother and father were separating because of her father's womanizing. Some nights Diana's father would not come home at all. Diana, though very young, knew that her father was cheating with other women and making her mother very angry. Diana would listen in on telephone calls of flirting and planning of hotels where her father would meet some of his women.

Diana and her mother left her father and went back to Louisiana. Her family had migrated from Weeks Island to a Parish called New Iberia, where Diana would enroll in her most memorable school and learn the southern life as her mother knew it. Diana liked school in New Iberia and all of the people in her school were either family or long-time friends. Most of the teachers had been her mother's teachers or were a good friend of the family or related some how. Diana's straight A's brought her honor and praise. She was called upon for almost everything in the school. Diana's mother and grandparents were very proud of her.

Diana began to love living home again. But something was missing. Diana danced, sang, cooked, cleaned, feed the animals, and made pillows, quilts, scarves, and she baked cookies, cakes, and pies all very well. She was and avid reader and an excellent speaker. Once she spoke at the church on behalf of the children's choir in a special children's program. Diana often spoke at the school programs. Diana could pick tomatoes, corn, greens, sugar cane and potatoes all evening and still have her homework done and then play outside too. She was so joyful and she made everything sound joyous. Diana sang in the church choir and played the piano. She loved to go to church on Sundays and entertain the congregation.

During all her years in New Iberia Diana developed a special relationship with the Lord. Diana so loved the Lord. She thought he was the greatest. She also pretended sometimes that she didn't need her real daddy because she had the Lord. God would take care of it. That was her favorite saying in times of trouble. Diana spent her quiet time talking to the Lord almost every day. Diana's grandfather believed that for a half hour each day everyone should have a quiet time. Diana enjoyed her talks and readings with the Lord. Diana's parents and grandparents were God fearing people. She developed an appreciation for peace and quiet for her mother and herself from her father's arguing. When Diana got calls from her daddy she would be so happy to hear from him. She remembered the long walks and the book readings that her father used to do with her as a baby. Diana wanted her mother and father to be able to live together and get along.

When Diana was seven, her father was again stationed at Walter Reed Army Medical Center and lived off base at the Dunbar Hotel. Diana's father had been begging her mother to come back to him so that they could be a family again. Diana's mother knew this would make Diana very happy so she agreed to give her marriage one more chance to work. When Diana came back to Washington, she had traveled all over the united states.
The kids in the school in Washington, D.C. were excited to play with Diana and hear her talk with her Louisiana accent, telling them about Los Angeles and New Iberia.

Diana's happy times did not last. Her mother was not happy for long. She found out that her husband had not changed and was still running with young women. They started arguing again and Diana began to feel sad to see her father come home sometimes. One morning Diana's father got dressed as if he was going to work and it was a normal day. He said, "I'll see you later Diana" and then left. Later Diana and her mother realized that some of his treasured items were gone. Diana's mother waited a few days and then called his Army Commander up and he told her that her husband had orders to go to Germany and that he thought she knew. Diana's mother was devastated and the commander could hear it in her voice how hurt she was. He told her that if she needed any help locating him that he would have his secretary help. Mrs. James asked to speak to his secretary. The secretary told her that her husband had been planning to leave for months and that he had taken his previous secretary with him. She said that she was sorry and gave Mrs. James the number to call to receive support until her husband was contacted. Mrs. James thanked her and said good-by. It was the summer season and Diana was getting older and understanding everything.

The year of 1968 would be a year of great pain for Diana for the rest of her life. One reason would be her father walking away without saying good-by and the other was the shocking death of Dr. Martin Luther King Jr. Diana would always remember the cries of the people and the smell of smoke burning everywhere. Diana and her mother were riding the bus down 8th and H Street, N.E. when they smelled the smoke of buildings burning. People were running from police and robbing stores. There were people standing around in discuss. There were news cameras and the news media everywhere. Diana was very young but she heard her mother speak with reverence about Dr. King so she had mixed feeling for what was going on around her. Diana felt very sad for Dr. King and his family but she also felt a mild sadness for the people that were burning their stores. You see, the stores on H Street were owned by either Blacks or Jews. Neither had killed Dr. King. She felt that in the long run the people would be sorry later. Some people said that the Jews that were burning their stores were very well insured and would be paid for damages. Black's were not as fortunate. Many Black owners lost their stores and their life savings in the fires. It was a tragedy all the way around. What was more confusing was that Dr. King was a nonviolent man, he preached and lived peace. He would have never approved of all that violence. One thing for sure, Dr. King was dead.

Many years later Diana would learn that the old saying her grandfather used to say "If you push a person too far, sooner or later he will retaliate." The Black people had been pushed too far. Another old saying her grandfather used to say was "If you get a group of Black people together and they start to think you can count on a blast."

These days were hard for Diana. Her father was gone, it was hard for her to go on. Diana was a loving child who loved her mother very much. She watched her mother make call after call to get money to support them. Diana's grandfather helped as much as he could. Diana's mother got help from social Service and they paid her rent for a smaller apartment on Quarrels Street, N.E. in Washington, D.C. Diana went to Davis Elementary School and was keeping her grades well above average in spite of her sadness. Diana's mother by this time was in nursing school and working for Walter Reed Army Medical Center, as a nurse's assistant. Diana's mother later became a registered nurse and got a permanent position at Walter Reed Army Medical Hospital.

Diana grew up with no sisters and brothers to look to for support in the new neighborhoods she moved to. She became friends with the characters in her books. She traveled to more than a dozen countries within books. Diana spent most of her time in school or reading. She became familiar with the lives of the characters in the books. Diana could feel the pain, hurt, and joy of the people in the books. Her life was the books she read. It was all she had except the dream that someday her father would come back to her. The pain of her father leaving was holding a special place in her heart. Diana controlled the pain so that it didn't show or take over her. Most of her days were pleasant and some were bright. Diana made the best of any and all situations. She had so much to remember and to hold on to. Her memory kept her going strong.

Almost everyone who met Diana was amazed at her beauty. But Diana never gave it much thought, she had learned along time ago that beauty was from within. In the south you were judged by your character and kindness not by your physical looks. Diana loved people and thought life was full of love and happiness. The years to come would prove hurt was inevitable and came in different degrees.

HARTFORD STREET, S.E.

In 1972 Diana and her mother moved to 2301 Hartford Street, S.E. in Washington, D.C. , the heart of the District of Columbia. Mrs. James, Diana's mother had received public assistance and she understood what it was like to live on a fixed income in fixed housing areas, and she wanted more for Diana. By now Diana's mother had a good job with moderate pay. The duplex building that Diana and her mother moved in was red brick on the outside. In the front of the duplex was six doorways, two facing you as you walked up the steep stairs to get to the buildings. Then there was two doorways you either walked right or left. There were only two apartments in each building. The red bricks connected all six buildings together. In front the steep steps had a long black medal rail going up on each side of the stairway. At the top the front had eight trees spread along the buildings.

As you walked into Diana's apartment the living room was facing you. It had stairs on the right that led to the two bedrooms and the one bathroom was directly at the top of the stairs. If you kept straight, the kitchen was in the back of the living room. The kitchen had a back door that led to the side of the building. Diana's room was painted pink with a twin-size bed and one pillow. She had a pink bed spread with a matching set of curtains and a black doll with a pretty lace pink dress sitting on the bed. There was only one dresser with three drawers. On the dresser was a musical jewelry box that her father gave her from Korea. Diana had lots of gifts that her father had given her as a child. She also had a good wardrobe of clothes and a closet that was half full and three pairs of shoes. Hartford Street was beginning to feel comfortable.

Diana walked and talked a little too "proper" for the other kids who had been born and raised in the ghetto. The first lesson

Diana got was learning that people don't take kindly to people they don't understand or people who are different. Her first day at Stanton Elementary School she was jumped and beat up on by some girls who did not understand that she was from a different area and that was why she talked and walked different and not because she was trying to be cool. Diana went home in tears that day. She did not understand how girls could act that way. The girls, victims themselves, turned to inflicting pain on others to overcome their misery and to keep their minds off the drugs they took and the run down areas they lived in. Most of them had mothers who were street walkers and or drug users. They were not taught love, peace, or kindness.

Diana tried to think about what happened in a logical sense. The next day she returned to school again hoping the girls were satisfied with beating on her for one day. But Diana was soon introduced to another kind of hurt. It was not enough that the girls had gotten away with the first day of beating Diana; they had planned to do it again. Diana was a strong little person with a sense of understanding and a long background, so when Diana heard this she decided to go to the biggest of the girls and fight her hoping she could win and they would all leave her alone. It worked. Diana offered the largest of the girls to fight one on one and she said no. The other girls were just followers. After that, the girls decided to leave her alone. Diana had began to make a name and a place for herself in the new neighborhood and she liked it.

But Diana was still different in so many ways. She had to be in the house before dark and clean the house before her mother came home. Cleaning and working were no strangers to Diana because she had worked on her grandfathers farm for so long and was use to hard work. She also had to do her homework and wait until her mother checked it before she went outside. Diana was so far advanced over her classmates that she would finish most of her homework before she got home. The curriculum in the southern states were advanced over the city curriculum. Diana was also a good helper for slower learners. The teachers always looked to Diana for help with the other students. That gave her very little time to be hanging out. Her mother was very strict and old fashioned in raising her. Diana could not come and go as she pleased. Her mother always knew where she was, what time she was coming back and who she was going with. Diana could not go to parties at night or school dances. She had to hear about them from her friends.

Diana was like a star, it's always shinning and bright and it's just there. She would dream a lot when most of her friends were out finding themselves. Diana loved to see the summer coming because it meant she had know homework and more time to be with the neighborhood kids. Diana would tell stories of her life in the other states and the stories her daddy had told her about other countries. The girls loved to hear the excitement in Diana's voice when she talked.

Diana once told the girls of a limousine that drove down her street with a movie star in it when she lived in LA. She told them that this tall blond got out with a white mink coat and diamonds every where. Diana said, "I remembered thinking how beautiful the lady was dressed and how special she must have been." Then one of the girls said, "I wish I could have been the white girl." Diana stood up and said, "Never wish you were white. You have so much culture and history in the black race to be proud of. There are so many stars in the black race who are succeeding and you can succeed too. My daddy used to say <u>If you can believe it and see it than you can do it.</u> He said that <u>All things are possible.</u> No, I never wished I was the white girl in the limo. I wished it were me as a black girl in the limo."

She then expressed how proud she was to be black. Diana

23

went on to tell more stories of her past experiences, some good and some bad. The girls listened and asked questions. Before it became dark outside at night Diana would have learned and played many games with the neighborhood kids. The joke among the kids was that Diana had to be in before the street lights came on. Mrs. James felt that no child should be out when the sun was gone in. If Diana was not there she would get her belt and go out calling for her. Diana did not want that, so she was in most of the time before dark.

Diana had long coal black hair like most southerners. She wanted to cut it when she was in the sixth grade but her mother said she was too young and that she could cut it when she got to the seventh grade. One year later when Diana was in the seventh grade at Krammer Junior High School, she did just that - cut her hair to shoulder length. Mrs. James was disappointed because she wanted to remember the little girl that used to scream and call on her daddy when she had to get her hair combed at night. But that little girl was fading quickly.

Diana was excited about going to junior high school and Krammer Junior High was as exciting as Diana dreamed it would be. She met new friends from far outside of her neighborhood. She met boys and girls and she was also introduced to girls with boy friends and boys who wanted to be her boy friend.
Diana knew her mother would not approve of her having a boy friend so she never thought of boys in that sense and played dumb-founded when they approached her about going together.

Diana's mother once came in and saw her talking to a classmate about homework at the door and slapped her in the mouth and slammed the door on the boy. Diana never forgot that.

She made it through the seventh grade with ease. It was the summer before the eighth grade and Diana was looking forward to going to her grandparents for three week and then spending the rest of the summer with her friends.

While Diana was in Louisiana she visited all of her relatives. She played softball with her cousins in the park and danced at night in the center. Diana loved being with her cousins and hanging out in the park. They would ride with carloads of people to the games in one car. Diana drove tractors and cars, so she would take her grandfather's truck sometimes when they were short of space in the other cars. Diana and her cousins would sit around until early morning hours talking and sharing information with each other.

While Diana was gone to visit her grandparents her friends at home missed her. Diana was like a breath of fresh air. Everywhere she went people loved her. After she returned from her trip she decided to spend as much time as she could with her friends. Diana had a best friend named Renee', a girl she befriended as soon as she moved to Hartford Street. They shared almost everything. They talked and shared secrets, reporting and comparing information on a day-to-day bases. Diana lived at 2301 Hartford Street and Renee' lived at 2305 Hartford Street. But although they lived close to each other, they had two different worlds, in which they shared. Diana told Renee' all she did in the south and Renee' told Diana what had happened in the neighborhood. Renee' told Diana that she had started to like a boy named Darrell and that they would talk on the phone a lot.

Diana enjoyed hearing all about Darrell. Darrell was the most popular boy on the Hartford Street and Irving Street side of the city. All the girls in the area had either gone with Darrell or wanted to go with him. He was very good looking and cool. He was from a big family with lots of older brothers. Renee' talked so much about Darrell that Diana felt as if she knew him personally. When Diana first met Darrell he liked her too. Darrell always talked about how pretty Diana was, which made Diana feel very uncomfortable. At first, Renee' did not mind. She also thought Diana was pretty, and did not realize Darrell was not making his comments lightly. Darrell would start to ask if Diana could go everywhere with Renee' and him. Diana would always make an excuse not to go. She did not know how to tell Renee' that Darrell was trying to talk to her.

Diana let it go and continued to be Renee's good friend, but slowly Renee' caught on and started staying away from Diana. Diana thought maybe it was best and did not question Renee', though she missed the long talks and walks that they would take. Diana's view of friendship was forever. The other kids came out to hear Diana talk and laughed all day, but it wasn't the same. She missed Renee'.

Diana was again drawn back to the characters in the books she read, because of the hurt from loosing her friend Renee'. She began to spend less time outside and more time reading.

2301 Hartford Street would be the beginning of a new life for Diana James. One that would center the rest of her life. Diana was a princess in the rough.

DIANA MEETS A BOYFRIEND

It was time to start the eighth grade and Diana was excited as ever about starting the new school year. She was still an honor roll student. One day Diana was sitting on the front steps of Krammer Jr. High during lunch when she noticed a boy standing on the front of the school steps. She looked at him closely to be sure that she was not seeing things. Diana then could not catch her breath, it was like she wanted to move but couldn't. She wanted to say something and the words did not come out. He reminded her of one of the characters in a book that she had read. Diana looked to the right again where he was standing, and could not turn her head from that direction. She was almost in shock that he was standing there. He was neat, good looking as in tall -dark-handsome, well dressed, well liked, mannerly, and cool. His name was Junior.

He noticed Diana too, but not in the way she noticed him. He was in the same grade with Diana and had been there last year, but she never noticed him then. Junior was from a middle class family. He lived in a house off of Gaylord and Gainsville Street, S.E. across from Hartford Street. The kids across Alabama Avenue where Diana lived were intimidated by the middle class kids. All the girls liked him because he was so good looking and cool. He did all the things most boys did in the 70s, like shoot dice, smoke marijuana, drink, party, sex, and hang in gangs. Complete opposite of what Diana dreamed of and now she could not stop dreaming of this one boy. He knew of the feelings Diana had for him because she would get so nervous when he was around. Diana dreamed of him every night almost all night, she looked forward to going to bed so she could dream of him. She hardly came outside because she was daydreaming of him all the time.

The summer came and Diana's mother said she could join the softball team of the neighborhood. The games were during the day so Diana was now allowed out the house before her mother got home from work. Diana was growing up.

One summer day the talk of the neighborhood was that Hartford Street was going to play Gainsville Street and that they were a rival team. Diana was so excited at the chance that Junior would be there and he was. Diana had on a pair of yellow jean shorts with a cotton white blouse and white tennis shoes. She looked beautiful, neat and clean and she planned her game well. She would look good on the team. She wanted to look sexy and innocent and at the same time inviting. Diana was all that and more.

Hartford Street team won the came thirteen to five. Diana was the star of the game and everyone loved her. Diana scored four of the thirteen runs and two of them were home runs. The game was a hit for the team. She was a star to her team and admired by the other team.

Diana and some girls were sitting on the bench talking about the game when Junior walked up. Diana was listening to the girls and did not see him walking up. He said, "Diana can I rap to you for a minute?" Diana was so shocked that she just stared at him without an answer at first. Junior was so sure of himself that he reached for Diana's hand and led her about ten steps away. Then she said "Sure, what can I do for you?" He said "Go out with me and we'll take it from there." He never let go of Diana's hand and she never moved her hand away.

Diana was remembering from all her dreams how good it felt when he touched her. His eyes were as beautiful as she dreamed them to be. He was kind and gentle speaking and at the same time sure of himself. When Diana finally spoke she said that she was honored that he had asked but no thank you. Diana then

28

removed her hand from his hand and said good-by.

Junior did not understand. He stood there surprised at what Diana had just said. Most girls jumped at his feet without him asking. But Diana's mother would not allow a date or boyfriend and Diana knew it. Diana said good-by and went back to talking to the girls. They walked home talking about the game.

Diana was so hurt that she did not come out for several days, dreaming and thinking that she had lost her first and only love. She had touched him and he had touched her. Now Diana had more to dream about. She loved him more after her brief encounter with him.

Diana was getting ready for school and preparing for her last year in Junior High School one August day when some of her friends came over and asked her to come outside and talk for a while. They did not understand why Diana had cut them off and stopped coming around. Diana had been teaching them the things she learned from her mother and father about foreign countries. The girls missed Diana's wisdom and stern up-bringing. One of the girls said, "Diana we heard you turned Junior down for a date last month. I thought you liked him. He is not the kind of guy you turn down and expect him to come back to you. I would have giving my right arm for that chance." Diana said in a soft meek tone, "Maybe you will get the chance one day." The girl went on to say that Junior was going out with a girl name Sharon. It hurt so bad to hear that, that Diana said to the girls, "I will see you all tomorrow." The girls sensed something was wrong and said, "later." Diana cried all night.

The next day she got up and did her housework. She had just started reading a book called **Black Boy,** by Richard Wright when the phone rang. It was a boys voice, asking for Diana. She recognized Junior's voice, "This is she," she answered, Junior paused for a minute and said, "Diana I have not seen you

29

in weeks and I have been coming on your street for days to see if I saw you. " He said, "Don't talk just listen. I have not been able to sleep since that day at the game and I feel so different. I feel like I need to see you before I can go on. I know this may sound strange. I really don't understand myself. I just feel it. At first I thought it was because I had never been turned down by a girl before. Then I realized it was you. It was you who had this affect on me. I needed to see or hear your voice before I could go on with my life. I don't think I ever missed anyone more than I have missed you these last few weeks. I have been out with other girls and out with the guys but it is not the same. Something is not right in my life. My parents asked me, who is this girl that could have changed me to this point. Please come by my house tomorrow and let's talk, please?"

Diana said yes, but I can't stay long. I will be there at twelve o'clock noon.

Junior said, "Thank you." Good-by. He asked Diana over to see if he was different because she had been the first girl to say no to him, or if something else was wrong.

That night Diana did not sleep, thinking of what it would be like to meet Junior's parents.

The next day was a Saturday and Diana got up early knowing her mother would think there was a game that day. Diana walked down Hartford Street and down Knox Place then over to Gainsville to Junior's house. She felt as if she had been there before, she had dreamed about it so much.

When Diana rang the doorbell Junior answered. When he opened the door he stared at how beautiful Diana was. He was thinking out loud, "I knew you were pretty but I didn't know you were that pretty." He took her hands, noticing how soft and pretty they were and lead her in the house. Junior said, "Thank you for coming," and Diana said "Thank you for calling." At this point Junior's mother and father walked into the living room and said, "Hello Diana! We have been expecting you and you are prettier than we expected." His father said, "Son if you are not in love with her, I am." They all smiled. Junior's mother, Delores Tolson, was a middle aged brown skinned women in her forties with a light grayish tint in the front of her hair. She was medium height with a slender built body. She was dressed in a silk pants suit with diamonds on both hands. Her smile was warm and friendly as she served lemonade and chocolate chip cookies with delight. His father, James Tolson, Senior was tall dark and handsome and his son looked just like him. They both had that charming voice and seemed to always no just what to say.

Diana was thinking, these people are doing well. She worried that they would not understand her life style. How could she explain?"

Diana did just that. She told how her father left with his secretary and her mother had to get help from public assistance and go to school to learn a trade. She told how they went from having everything to nothing. When Diana finished talking they loved her even more for being the beautiful person she was despite the odds.

If Junior was not in love with Diana before he was now and he knew it. Diana told Junior about how she felt about him the first day she saw him and he was thrilled. He took Diana out in the back yard and said, "I know now that the reason I could not go on was because I love you and I can't be without you. Please be my girlfriend." Diana said, "Thank you, but I could never be the kind of girl you should have, I can't go out or even have boys over and I can't be with you the way Sharon can. It would not be fair to you to pretend I could be your girlfriend when I can't." Diana started walking away and he walked after her and said, "I can wait, I will wait, I will never stop loving you or wanting you, so I will wait until you are ready. " Diana never said that it was her mother who would not allow her to go out but somehow Junior sensed it and did not want to pressure her.

When she turned around she was crying and Junior kissed her and held her in his arms, and it felt so good that she kissed him back the way she did so many times in her dreams. Junior's father owned a small dry cleaners and was living large. He had an air about him with his money that Diana had without money and he recognized her air.

As Junior was holding Diana, Veny Mason, Junior's next door neighbor and childhood friend, came up to the fence and asked Junior what he was doing with Diana. Veny was upset and she started screaming she thought she was going to be Junior's girlfriend. Diana understood her hurt and sent Junior over to her. She said that she would wait in the house for Junior while he talked to Veny and then he could walk her home. Diana did not know what Junior told Veny, but she knew she wanted Junior and it would take more than Veny to stop her. Junior and Diana talked as he walked her home that evening and promised to wait for her until she was ready.

He met some of his friends along the way and they were congratulating him on his latest fling and saying that Diana was the best looking of them all. He ignored them looking into Diana's eyes thinking how much he loved her. When Diana got to the bottom of her steps she said good-by and thank you again to Junior as he kissed her and let go of her hand. Junior said good-by and walked back to his friends on the corner. Diana was so happy that she felt as though she were sleeping night and day. Diana talked to Junior every day on the phone and sometimes twice a day. They talked about school, mutual friends, family, love, and the time they would spend together. They fell more and more in love by the days. Diana had become a favorite of Junior's parents also.

September came and it was time for school. Diana was excited because she knew she could see Junior throughout the day. She was eager to go to the ninth grade, but even more eager to see Junior. Diana did not know that they would drift apart from girls and boys telling her the things Junior was doing while she was in the house. He was going out with girls, drinking, doing drugs, and even selling from time to time. Diana did not know this part of the guy she had falling in love with. Junior was another person when he talked to Diana. When Diana asked him about it, Junior would say, "Don't believe what you hear, it is you I love baby." Junior was telling the truth about loving Diana, but he was doing some of everything while waiting for her.

Diana was homecoming queen and president of her class. Her school work kept her busy and Junior knew that.

One day when Diana and Junior was talking at lunch a girl came up and said, "Junior will you be staying at my house tonight again?" Junior wanted to die. Diana said to him, "Maybe this was a bad idea for us to commit to each other at so young. I understand what you are used to in girls and I can't give it to you, so I am releasing you to go on with your life, and if our love is strong enough than we will be together later. But for now please don't call me anymore." Diana was so hurt she started to cry. Junior gave her his handkerchief and said "I love you." Diana said "I love you too, please go. Its better if we stop now than later. It will hurt more later." Junior went home. He was so hurt. Diana missed his calls but unplugged her phone so that he could not call her.

After a while Junior went on but he never forgot Diana, he tried to make every girl he came into contact with be Diana and it did not work. Junior's mother and father also missed Diana's calls and constantly scolded him about losing her. Diana finished the year with straight A's and a broken heart. It helped that she knew Junior loved her still.

Diana and Renee' started talking again and Diana was happy that she had her friend again. Diana shared with Renee' all the pain and hurt she was feeling. Renee' was heavily involved with her boyfriend Darrell and spent even less time with Diana. Their short times together were for talking sessions only.

Diana was sad about Junior but went on with her life. Junior never stopped calling to tell Diana he loved her. Diana would talk sometimes and other times she would say she was busy.

It was the end of the school year and Diana had finished with honor's. Her mother was so proud of her. Junior's parents, whom she talked to from time to time were proud of Diana also. They had started to look at her as part of the family. She was included in all their celebrations and gatherings. Junior was always glad to be able to be with Diana at his cookouts or family gatherings. He knew his mother would always ask Diana to come and he would always be there to get a chance to hold her or touch her. Diana would always take pictures for Junior and he had them in his bedroom and in his living room. His parents loved Diana very much. Everyone in S.E. Washington knew that Junior loved Diana. He made it clear to all the girls he messed around with that Diana was his girlfriend and that she was who he loved. Diana knew he loved her and that she was special to the whole family. It was a good feeling to be loved and accepted into a real family. One that had a father and a mother. Diana would always tell Junior how lucky he was to have both parents with him.

Diana was leaving for L.A. on Monday and it was a Friday afternoon when Juniors mother called and asked Diana to come over for a cookout on Saturday and Diana said she would be there. Diana got there after some of the guest and Junior was talking with his cousins when Diana walked in. Junior's mother grabbed Diana's hand and took her around to some friends and introduced her as her daughter. Diana was very flattered and shocked. It was a pleasant surprise. After Junior's mother took Diana all around to everyone, Junior walked over and said "Hi, beautiful." Diana said "Hi." Junior said "Come with me and let me talk to you." Everyone watched as Diana and Junior walked into his room. Diana felt people would think that they were going to do something and she was embarrassed about being in there. After Junior closed the door and kissed Diana she felt more comfortable. She forgot about the people outside the door. Junior said to her "I have waited so long to kiss you, I miss you so much." Diana said "I miss you, too." Then she said "Jay, I need to tell you something." He said "Call me Jay again." Diana said "Why?" He said "Because know one has ever made my name sound so good like that before but my mother and you. I like it when you say it." Diana smiled and said "That's because I think you are so special and I love you." Then Diana said, "I will be leaving for L.A. on Monday and I will be gone for three weeks. I will miss you. I wanted you to know that I love you and I will be thinking about you." Junior said "Is there any way I can stop this trip?" and she said, "No." "Please Jay take care of yourself." He said "At least we can spend the day together before you leave." "No, I have to go with my mother somewhere at three o'clock so I have to leave soon", Diana replied. "I have already said good-by to your parents last week. They need you as much as I do, so please be careful." Junior held Diana for about ten minutes just standing there holding her repeating "I love you baby." At that time Junior's mother was calling Diana to meet someone else. Jay watched Diana for one hour as she smiled and laughed with his family members as he was hurting so bad because she was leaving. Diana sat by Jay every chance she got and he kissed her the hold time she was near him. Diana asked Jay to take her home and they left. Jay was driving now and he used his father's car as if it were his. He drove to the movies, parties, and to pick-up friends. On the way to taking Diana home Jay stopped one block from Diana's apartment building and kissed Diana good-by one last time. They held each other and then Jay drove Diana in front of her apartment. Diana got out and waved by. When Junior got back to his house he went to his room to be alone. His mother walked in and said, I know how you feel. I miss her to when she is not here. She will be back and you two will be together. You need the time from her and she needs the time from you." He said, "Mother I love her so much." She hugged him and said "I know son." Junior then came out to be with his cousins, never forgetting Diana's last touch and their good-by kiss. Diana and Jay were really in love. Their love would be tested to the extreme in the months to come.

SUMMER IN L.A.

The summer Diana went to L.A. to visit her cousins. Diana wrote Junior a six-page letter telling him that she did not blame him for what happened and that it was her fault. She said that she tried to make her dreams reality using him, then she asked if they could be friends next year and support each other in Senior High.

L.A. was a faster growing place than D.C. an Diana's cousins had boyfriends calling on them, so when Diana's mother came and saw that she was dating in L.A. she agreed to let Diana Date in D.C.

Diana was having a good time in L.A. She saw old friends and made new friends. Diana visited museums and family. She was very busy. Diana had met a guy name Derrick. Derrick lived on the same block as her cousin's that she was staying with. He was good looking and tall with smooth skin and curly hair. Derrick was a little older than Diana, so he knew how to treat her. He sent her flowers and bought candy for her. He also drove a sporty car and gave her long rides in it. Derrick was in college at Southern University and he was home for the summer. They went out while Diana was in L.A. Diana told Junior about Derrick and the fact that she could entertain at home now and Junior was happy Diana could date but disappointed that Derrick was such a nice guy. Diana did not put a return address on her letter because she did not want Junior to write her back. She wanted Jay to go on with his summer and not try to contact her.

Diana visited her aunt on her father's side. She took her cousins and Derrick with her one time. Diana's aunt believed in palm readings. She prided herself on never being wrong on foretelling someone's future. Diana on this day let her read her

37

palm. Diana's aunt told her that she could see the hurt deep down in her of her father's leaving. She said, There are a lot of mixed emotions about your father." Diana asked her aunt to go on to something else because she did not want to think about her father now. Diana's aunt went on with the reading. She told Diana that she would be involved with a prince and that he will love you more than life itself. He will take care of you for the rest of your life. Diana asked what was his name. She said, "I don't know." Diana's aunt told her to just follow her heart. Diana did not know who this prince was or even if she believed there was one. She only knew that she loved Jay. She told her aunt that it was time to go and that she was glad to be able to visit with her. They said good-by and Diana and her company left.

The next day Derrick came over to take Diana to the park and he asked her to stay. He said that he had fallen in love with her. Then he told her that he would take care of her forever if she stayed in L.A. Diana said "Thank you, that is nice, but I am in love with a guy name Jay who lives in D.C." She thanked him for a good time and wished him luck in life. Diana was leaving the next day. Derrick was sad but he tried to let Diana go in peace. The day Diana left he called to ask Diana to think about staying with him. She said "No." Diana's cousin and Derrick drove her to the airport later that day. They were all going to miss her very much. The three weeks they had spent together were full of fun. And now it was time to go back to her real love.

When Diana was in L.A. Junior was becoming a big time drug dealer and a ladies man. He had no control over his role in a S.E. drug label. Junior was the most admired young boy in the neighborhood. He had a reputation for protecting himself and the people he loved. Everybody knew he loved Diana and that he would kill if anything happened to her.

Diana returned home a different girl. Junior was a different person too. Diana had liked another boy who was kind to her, but

38

she did not like him like she loved Junior. But her love would not be easy to bear in the days ahead. Diana called Junior the day she got home and he was not there so she talked to his mother and told her that she had something for them and that she would bring it over tomorrow. The next day when Diana got there Junior had a girl there and she was very pretty. Junior was in the kitchen with her. Junior's mother did not know the girl was there and was so hurt for Diana. Diana was hurt and surprise, she said that it was alright and that she could not stay anyway she just wanted to drop the gifts off. Junior immediately ran to her and said he loved her and that he was sorry. Diana slapped him and said "If you loved me you would not have been with someone else while I was thinking of you." She ran away in tears.

Junior got dressed and took the girl home and ran after Diana. When he caught up with her it was twenty minutes later and Diana was at her house in the living room crying her eyes out. When Junior knocked at the door Diana asked him to go away and said that she did not feel good. She asked him if they could talk tomorrow. Junior said that he could not go without talking to her. Diana said "Please Jay leave me alone." Jay then told her that he loved her and that he needed her to know it.

Diana opened the door and as Jay was walking in, he could see the tears on her face. He took his hand and wiped her tears and said, "Baby I never knew how much I loved you until I saw you hurting like you are now. It hurts so bad to know that you are hurting and that I caused the pain. I have done a lot of things in my life time that I am not proud of. But the one thing that I regret most is the hurt you are feeling now." He paused and said, "Diana I am so sorry, please forgive me. I love you so much I need to know that you know it." Jay reached for Diana and he held her for a while without saying a word. When Diana spoke she said, ":Baby I love you too. I missed you so much. You are all I could think of while I was away. Coming back to you is what I dreamed of every night. Our love for each other is so strong that we can workout any problems." "Jay I have to ask you, do you care about her, the girl I saw you with?" He said, "no, I tried to make her you, like I have done with every girl that I have met since I have known you. What ever you need, I am here for you."

Drugs were in the ghetto and they were a new hope for the under worked. They became a way of survival, a way to feed your family. Drugs provided a way for the luxuries that jobs did not pay enough for. It almost seemed unreasonable to tell a man not to sell drugs to feed his hungry child. In the ghetto men were told that they could not get jobs but selling drugs were wrong. Drugs were a way out of the ghetto for most people who sold them. Drugs were the answer to the rent man; they meant food, clothes and good times. Later they would prove to be worst than we could have ever imagined. They would break-up families, change people's minds, morals, and ethics. They would start a conspiracy against black males. The drugs would bring death and hopelessness. The fate of young black men, some only boys would later become a destruction.

Diana was totally against drugs and she preached to Jay all the time about how drugs would destroy the neighborhood. Diana saw what they made mothers and fathers do to their kids. She saw husbands turn their wives into street walkers. She spent most of her time showing Jay how the drugs were a form of enslavement. Jay always saw the drugs the way Diana saw them until she was out of sight. The chains from the drugs were much stronger than Diana at this point.

Junior was driving a 1975 Toyota Celica now before it hit the dealers good. Jay told Diana how much he missed her and that he did love her but the drugs were taking over his body. Diana hugged and kissed him and then asked if he needed help, and he told her that he did. Diana agreed to help him if he wanted to really get away from the drug scene. Junior told her that he did. Diana went to counseling with Junior three nights a week and walked, talked and held him through this difficult time and junior loved her more for it.

Junior changed, he kept a low profile the rest of the summer and he spent as much time with Diana as he could. He loved her and did not want to lose her. Diana loved him and did not want to lose him. Junior stopped using drugs and spent more time reading or listening to Diana read. On Saturdays they would go downtown on the bus and visit museums on Independence Avenue, N.W.

One Saturday Jay took Diana to see the Washington Monument and the Lincoln Memorial. They walked from L'nfant Plaza to the Monument and then down to the Lincoln Memorial. They walked all day holding hands and kissing each other. When Diana looked up it was getting late and then they walked back to the bus stop on Seventh street to catch the bus home. As they walked pass Knox Place and up Hartford Street they passed a lot of Jay's old friends. The guys were asking Jay where had he been. Jay said, "Laying low with my baby." Diana kissed him and said "Baby lets go." Jay said to the guys, I'll catch you later." When they got to Diana's house her mother was just going in the house from work. Junior had gotten to know Diana's mother very well and he also began to love her strict rules. Diana was happy that Junior loved her mother. She and Junior spent all day together and woke up to be with each other and for one month there were no other girls or drugs. The next few years would prove that love conquers all.

1975 ANACOSTIA HIGH SCHOOL

It was now September 1975 and Diana and Junior's first year in high school. Junior was already well known around Anacostia High School because he sold drugs to a lot of the older students. But Diana didn't let this worry her; she was just glad to be there with Junior. He would pick Diana up for school every morning and stay with her until late at night before going home for the first month of high school. By October Junior was dropping Diana home and saying he would be back later. Diana would call his house and he would not be there and when she saw him he would lie about where he was spending his time. Diana felt there was someone else and she did not want to hold Junior back so she asked him not to pick her up anymore and to feel free to see other girls. Junior said no, but she insisted to the point where he just gave in. Diana asked him not to test her love again.

Anacostia was famous during the year 1975 because it had a good football team and a excellent basketball team. Diana was well known in the school for her grades and her popularity. She was the prettiest girl in the school, and the best-dressed sophomore. Junior would take Diana shopping every weekend and buy her all kinds of pretty clothes. He loved buying her lingerie, and dreaming of how she would look in each item he bought her, and hoped that he could see someday. Diana showed the teachers what helped her achieve academically and suggested that they tried teaching as friends. The teachers appreciated her help. She was always willing to help. She was on all the committees that was going on in the school. She organized, protested, and demonstrated whenever it was necessary.

Diana was sitting on the front porch of Anacostia high one evening when Jay drove up and parked his car. Jay walked over and asked Diana to come with him. Diana said no that she had rehearsal for a play in one hour. He said okay, I'll come back in two hours and pick you up. Diana said, "no, I already have a ride, thank you. I will call you later."

Jay walked close up to Diana and kissed her and said "Later".

Diana watched Jay drive off with some of his friends and then went into the school to prepare for the rehearsal. After the rehearsal some friends dropped Diana off in front of her apartment.

Diana walked slowly up the stairs enjoying the fresh air on a cool spring night. As she was approaching her apartment her friend Renee' came out and called her. Renee' asked Diana if she was alright. Diana said, "I am fine, thank you." Renee' asked Diana if they could talk and Diana said yes. They sat on Diana's porch for two hours talking. As usual Renee' told Diana what was going on with her and Darrell and Diana told Renee' what was going on with her and Jay. That was how it was with these two friends. They both would comfort each other in their times of sorrow.

That night, Diana said to Renee', "I am so glad that you are my friend. If nothing else comes out good in this life of mine, you have been my friend through it all." Diana asked Renee' to spend Saturday with her talking and laughing all day. Renee' agreed, adding that they were going to be "medicine" for each other. Diana told Renee' that she had to get up early the next day for another rehearsal so she had to go to bed now. Renee' said "good night and thanks for being my friend." Diana said "Thank you too."

Diana was not in the house five minutes before she got a call from Jay. He said he wanted to see her and he was on his way over. Diana said, "No! Jay, I'm tired and I am going to bed." Jay said, "This will only take a minute. Please Diana." Then she agreed. Jay came over twenty minutes later. When Diana opened the door Jay had two dozen roses. Diana said, "You shouldn't have. Thank You. Jay!" Jay said, "I love you and I feel you

43

drifting away." Diana said, "We both should try to go on and just be friends." Jay said, "I love you and I don't want to be just friends." Diana said ,"Is that what you tell the other girls that you are with at night?" Jay shocked that Diana knew what he was doing behind her back with other girls. He said, "No, I tell them how much I love you and I try to make them you. I love you." Diana said, "Please Jay, I am tired. Go on with your life and save those lines for your girls." Jay said, "Diana please tell me you still love me, it's the only way I can go on. Diana said, "Jay I love you and I miss you, but, I understand you need more. If we were meant to be we will meet again later in life." Jay said, "I love you baby." Diana said, "Good-by, Jay." He left feeling happy because he knew in his heart Diana still loved him.

Diana continued to go to school and do well. Jay was in and out of school all year. Only, he spent more time out than in. Jay was able to come back and catch up with his class after being out for a while. The teachers had a great respect for him because of his popularity. They were also intrigued by his charm and good looks. The male teachers amused by his cool style.

At last the night of the talent show came. Under Diana's direction, the talent and fashion show closed the school year out. The night of the show Jay picked Diana up to take her to the school. He could not take his eyes off Diana because she was even more beautiful than usual. She was wearing a gold dress that fit tightly and it was way above her knee. She was wearing shoes to match the dress. Diana and two other students sang a song in the show called "Bad Whether." The song was a hit and so was the show.

The talent show featured beautiful clothes. Diana wore two lovely gowns. Every guy in the school who didn't already love Diana fell in love with her that night. Jay was there and he stuck close by Diana. He could feel the other guys falling in love with "his girl." He was very protective of Diana.

After the show Jay took Diana home and they talked all night until the dawn. Jay told Diana how much he loved her and needed her. He told Diana at least a hundred times how beautiful she looked that night. Diana thanked him for taking and bringing her home from the show. Jay asked her if he could kiss her and Diana said, "No." She told him that it would put pressure on the both of them and that they did not need the pressure that a kiss would bring. Diana listened to Jay talk and talk. He told her of the dreams he had for both of them in the future. Diana could not see Jay's dreams because she felt that she and Jay were drifting apart. Diana said to Jay that she was getting sleepy and that she would see him the next day. Jay said, "Baby please let me kiss you, I will not be able to go on until I kiss you. I love you, please baby let me hold you." Diana reached over and said, "Jay I love you so much." Then she kissed him lightly on his lips and he reached for her and kissed her back laying her seat down and rolling over on her. Diana said, "Jay please," but he did not stop, and it felt so good that Diana let him kiss and hold her. Diana then said "Jay thank you." He said, "I love you baby." Jay got out of his car and opened Diana's door and walked her up the stairs. He kissed her again at her door and said, "I'll dream of you tonight." Diana smiled and said, "Me too." Jay left and went home. When he got to his house he went straight to his room and called Diana. Diana and Jay talked for a while and then Diana said, "Good-night Jay. We can talk some more tomorrow." Jay said, "Good-night baby."

On the last day of school Diana got so many phone numbers from so many guys she could not keep up with all of them. Diana stayed later on the last day of school to help some teachers pack. Jay dropped by earlier to tell Diane he was taking her home that day and she asked him if he could come about five o'clock. He said he would.

Diana said good-by to all the teachers and waited for Jay on the front porch. Most of the students were gone. While Diana was waiting a well groomed, well mannered and good looking guy came up and said, "Hi you're Diana. I have watched you all year and you are special. Like all the other guys, I have fallen in love with you too." Diana smiled and said, "who are all these guys?" as if she could not see how they looked at her. "You are sweet." Diana said, "And you are nice." He said, "take my number and call me over the summer." As he was giving her the number, Jay pulled up. He parked his car and walked up to Diana and kissed her as if they were a couple. Diana said, "Jay, this is Mayo, Mayo this is Jay." Jay said, "Hi." Then he looked at Diana and said "are you ready, baby?" Mayo said "Diana, good-by, and I hope to hear from you over the summer." Diana said, "Thank you, good-by."

Jay carried the folder that Diana put Mayo's number in along with a bunch of other numbers. He put the folder behind him so that he could reach it and Diana couldn't. He asked Diana as they were driving why was she talking to "that dude." Diana said, he was just a "guy," adding that he was nice and he thought I was nice. Besides it was just a conversation." Jay looked at Diana and said. "You should have told him that you had a boyfriend." Diana said, "Jay it's late. Please just take me home." Jay said, "After while. I need to talk to you." Diana said, "Can we talk tomorrow." Jay said, "No." He drove to Anacostia Park and parked his car by the water. Diana was beginning to get angry. She said Jay look, call one of your girlfriends and talk to her. I'm tired. Take me home Jay." Jay opened his car door and pulled the folder out and lit a match to the folder and it burned into ashes.

Now Diana was angry. "If you are finished, take me home." Jay said, "You will go home when I take you home. Diana you will not be needing those numbers because I am the only guy you will be calling." Diana never had time to think much about the girls Jay was with when she was not around, until now. She told Jay that he should spend more time with his other girls and leave her alone. She said, "Whatever we had has been over for a long time." Jay said, "Diana I love you and it will never be over." Diana said, "If you love me take me home. I know you are out with other girls and I don't even mention it because I love you to much to take the chance of loosing you. Jay I have had enough and I want to go on with my life. Please take me home." Jay said, "Yes, but I do everything I do because I love you. When ever I am not with you I get strength from knowing you love me. I need to hear you say you love me." Diana looked at Jay and knew that he did not hear a word she had said. She understood Jay was not going to accept anything less. Her words were soft, but firm. "Jay I love you so much. Whenever you are ready I'll be here for you." Jay hugged Diana and started to drive her home. He looked at his watch twice so Diana knew he had something to do. When Diana got home she said, "Jay, call me later. He said, "I love you, baby." Diana got out and grabbed her bag and said, "See you." Diana had the wisdom and the strength to save Jay. But would she?

JUNIOR DEALS DRUGS

The drug lords loved Junior also. He had made them big money in the summer that Diana was in LA and they did not forget it. Junior could easily have made one to two million dollars a year for the drug lords, and he did it in such a business like manner. If he had a chance to build a company of his own he could apply the same tactics and be equally successful. Economics was a natural instinct for him.

As he built his "career," Junior continued to call Diana and say he loved her. Diana would always love junior and she knew it, but she agreed to go out with another guy name Tony. One night, getting ready for their first date, Diana dressed in a multi colored silk dress with spaghetti straps, the V cut of the dress centered her breast.

Tony picked Diana up at seven o'clock sharp, Diana's dress was simply beautiful. Her shoes were satin with the matching bag. She was dressed like a movie star. They had dinner reservations at Blackie's House of Beef.

When Junior heard about this he went to the restaurant were Diana and Tony was having dinner. Jay drove up and parked in front of the restaurant and went in. He walked over to their table and Diana asked Jay what was he doing and he said, "I'm taking you home." She said, "Jay please. I'm having dinner with a friend." Diana asked her dinner date to excuse her while she talked to Jay. Jay then reached for Diana and her date stood up and asked Diana if she was alright. Jay reached over and punched the guy down. Then he picked Diana up put her in his car to take her home and when the guy tried to talk to him he hit him again and knocked him out.

Diana was so upset that she told junior that the only reason she never tried to hold him back from seeing other girls was because she knew that she was not ready to sleep with him and she understood that he needed sex. Diana asked him why would he humiliate her like that. Junior said, "Because I love you and the thought of you with someone else makes me want to give up, I need to know you still love me and that you are there for me." Diana said, "I do love you. It was just dinner and a talk." Junior said, I have know doubt that it was just dinner but I can't stand that either."

Diana said she loved him again and agreed to wait for him. Junior asked Diana for the first time to let him make love to her and Diana said, "You have never asked, and I hoped that you would not ask until you knew I was ready. I love you so much until I was afraid that I might give in, but thank God, I love you enough to say no, I am not ready. I am not ready for the responsibility of having sex.

Having sex would put a lot of stress on me. If we were having sex it would hurt so much more when I knew you were sleeping or even being with someone else. I love you enough to wait for you now, but if we had sex in our relationship I would not be as understanding as I have been. I believe that with having sex comes a responsibility to each other, trust, honor, and respect. Not only am I not ready for sex in our relationship but I do not think you are either. It would mean a total commitment to me. When the time comes for sex in our relationship we will both know it. Please understand." Junior said, "I do. I just wanted you to know that it is you I want to make love to, but because you are not ready I love you even more and you are more than worth waiting for. I love you Diana James." "I love you too, Junior."

Jay went home that night happy. Diana knew that he would be worth waiting for. Junior spent as much time with Diana as he could, but to run a million dollar drug business you have to spend a lot of time in the streets.

Diana was a sleep one summer night when she got a call from Junior's mother saying that junior had been stabbed and that he had been rushed to the hospital. She said that the car was left down the street from her house. Diana said that she had keys and would get the car and pick her up. It was one o'clock AM when Diana got dressed and walked to the car and drove to Junior's mother house to get her. It was one thirty AM when they arrived at D.C. General Hospital. The nurse who admitted Jay said that he had lost a lot of blood and was in surgery. Diana was terrified that Jay might die. She waited patiently with his mother trying to comfort her at times. Diana called her mother and said that she would be spending a night there at the hospital. The surgery was over by five o'clock AM, but Junior did not come to until eight o'clock that morning. Diana and Junior's mother were right there. Junior woke up and his first words were, "I'm sorry. You two are the two I love most in this world and I never wanted to hurt you." Jay's mother said, "Thank God you are alright. You scared us to death. I can finally breath now." She walked over to him and kissed him and said "I love you son." His mom left out the room to get the doctor.

Diana ran over to kiss Jay. "I love you so much, I know I can't go on without you, please don't ever leave me." Diana laid on Junior and cried. The doctor came in and said that Junior should sleep for four to five hours. Diana told Jay that she did not want to go without him. She held him and cried for five minutes. Then remembering his mother was there, she told him that she would be back soon as she took his mother home. Diana kissed Jay and left to take his mother home.

After taking his mother home and talking with her for a while Diana went home to try to sleep for a few hours. Later that day Jay called Diana and said that she did not have to come back that day and for her to get some sleep. Diana said she loved him and went to bed. Diana went to work in an elementary school during the day and visited Jay in the hospital at night. Junior was there for two weeks before the hospital released him to go home.

Diana picked Junior up from the hospital on the day that he was released. She took him home and put him in bed. She told him to get some rest and that she would be back the next day. The next day when Diana got to Jay's house he was up and dressed.

The talk of the neighborhood was that Junior was better and going out for revenge. Diana after hearing this ran to his house and begged him not to go. Junior was lifting weights and building his body up. He had lifted weights four days a week for most of his young life.

Diana told jay of the plans she had for them for the day. Jay said, "Later or tomorrow. I have a meeting now." Diana said, "I know where you are going. Please don't go." Diana asked him if it was true what she had heard, and he said yes. Diana said, "Than I am going with you. If you are going to die than I want to be with you." Junior smiled and said, "I love you." Diana got angry and said, If you love me then stay here and make love to me." Junior wanted that more than anything in this world but he knew Diana did not mean what she was saying. Diana unbuttoned her blouse and laid on Junior's bed and said, "Come here baby." Junior walked over sat beside her and kissed Diana and said "I love you but get up please before I can't say no. I'll take you home." Diana said, "No, I want to be here with your mother when they call and say you are dead." Junior walked out. Diana cried her eyes sore.

When Junior's mother came out of her room Diana told her that he went to take a friend home and that he would be back later. Junior's mother went to bed and Diana went to Junior's room to watch TV. Diana woke up at two AM and Junior was not home yet, so she put on his pajama shirt and went to bed. At four AM Junior came in and Diana heard him say, "I love you baby" and she went back to sleep. When Diana woke up Junior was beside her looking at her, he said, I have never loved this room or bed more than I do now." Diana said, "Thank you for being you." She was thanking him for not having sex with her before she was ready .

Junior got up and made Diana breakfast and Diana took a shower and started putting on her clothes when Junior walked in the room. She had her shirt open showing her white lace bra and was pulling up her jeans over her silk white panties when Junior came in the room and said, "Wait, I don't know how long it will be before I see your beautiful body again so please give me a minute now." He walked over and kissed Diana, rubbing his hands down her butt and across her breast. Diana just stood there until she felt what felt like a long fist rising against her and she said, "Baby what's that I smell cooking?" Then Junior opened his eyes and said, "Don't you want to know what was that you just felt?" Diana said "I know what that was, thank you, and I look forward to meeting that part of you." Diana said, "Baby I have to know. Did you kill him?" Jay said, "No I couldn't find him."

That same night the guy who stabbed Jay was shot to death. He had beat up two brother's the week before he stabbed Jay. They walked up on him from the back and shot him five times.

Junior wanted to marry Diana. He had asked her many times to run away and get married. So he planned to buy her a friendship ring the following Saturday and he did. It was one Karat with lots of color to it. Diana was so happy that she showed it to all her friends. It was the summer before it was time for Diana to go to the eleventh grade. That summer she played softball again for the Hartford Street team. Diana and Junior spent most of the days together and Junior was loving her more and more. The neighborhood recognized them as a couple. They looked and acted very much in love and everyone knew it.

ST. ELIZABETH HOSPITAL

It was the beginning of the eleventh grade for Diana and Junior at Anacostia High. The first week was hard and rushed for Diana, but finally she did settle down and got on schedule after helping everyone else in the school. Things were going great in school and with Jay. He was spending a lot of time with Diana day and night.

One night Diana's mother received a call that said her husband had been shell shock in Germany and was to be shipped back to Walter Reed Army Medical Center. Diana was so happy to hear the news of her father coming back that she immediately called Jay to tell him. He was not home. Diana told Jay's mother and they talked for an hour about what she was going to say to her father as soon as he got there, not knowing what condition her father was in. The call said that her mother should meet her father in St. Louis on the following Friday. Diana couldn't wait to see her father. Diana's Mother left on a Thursday and arrived in St. Louis that night. She called Diana to say that she had arrived and would call back the next day.

Saturday morning Diana got a call from her mother saying she would not be back until Monday because there was a doctor there who wanted to examine her father. Diana was puzzled but said, "Okay." She called and told Jay what was going on, and he asked Diana to sleep at his house so she would not be alone. Diana agreed.

When Diana arrived at Jay's house he wasn't there, so after helping with dinner Diana watched television until ten o'clock PM and then she told Jay's mother that she was tired and wanted to lie down. She went to Jay's room. Diana started to read and fell asleep. When Jay came in she was asleep and in his pajama shirt

53

again. Jay kissed her and said he was sorry but he got stuck in traffic coming from New York. "What were you doing in New York?" Diana asked, then Jay put his hand over her mouth and said "Don't talk, don't think, just relax," and she did that. Jay started kissing Diana and she loved the way it felt. He unbuttoned her (or should I say his pajama shirt) and continued to kiss her. He kissed her whole body, and it felt so good that she did not want to stop him and she didn't. As he was kissing her body he was taking off the pajama shirt. He kissed her feet and each toe, he caressed and kissed her until she had to scream. He made love to her until the sun came up and Diana loved him even more. The first time for Diana was perfect and it was even better than any movie they had watched. Diana knew that their love had been taking to a higher level.

They laid in bed until ten o'clock AM. Diana told Jay that she had never felt so good in all of her life and that she loved him for making her feel good. She said that she wanted to sleep with him every night for the rest of her life.

Diana and Jay took their first shower together and dressed in the same room for the first time. Later Jay took Diana home and together they waited for her mother's call. When she did call she said, that Diana's father was sick and would be leaving Walter Reed Army Medical Center after three days to report to Saint Elizabeth Hospital and he was not to have visitors for a while. St. Elizabeth Hospital was for the mentally ill and disturbed. Mrs. James told Diana that she would explain when she got there. Diana was crying so hard that as Jay was holding her she did not see he was tired from the night they spent together. When Diana did notice she asked him to leave so she could get some sleep. Jay kissed Diana and said "Call me if you need to. I will be home," and then he left.

Diana changed for bed and went to sleep. At two o'clock AM Jay called to say that he loved her and to see if Diana needed anything. Diana said that she loved him too and that she would call him in the morning.

A week passed before Diana's father could see her. Diana started to spend a lot of time with her father, getting to know him again. Junior spent a lot of time missing Diana and hanging in the streets.

Jay picked Diana up for school the first month and went to the hospital with her every evening for one month. But Diana did not want Jay to be spending time with her at the hospital when he wanted to be somewhere else. Also, she wanted to spend some time alone getting to know her father again. So one evening Diana told Jay that she felt he was not happy with her. She assured him that he didn't have to pick her up and bring her back and forth to the hospital anymore. She said that she still loved him. Junior said "Okay" so fast that it shocked Diana because he usually gave her no's and tried to talk her out of things but this time he just said "Okay."

Diana went into her house hurt. She knew she had lost him because he wanted his freedom. Diana would see Jay in school in passing and he would always hug and kiss her and say "I love you." But Diana knew it was different now. Junior knew that other guys were interested in Diana and it didn't bother him as much as it used to, or at least he didn't show it now. That hurt Diana also. But Diana loved Jay and was willing to wait for him to return to his old ways.

At the end of the year one of Junior's friends told Diana that Jay was into selling big time drugs and didn't want her to get hurt. Diane knew he loved her and was protecting her from his life. In the meantime Diana was spending time with her father at the hospital. She would go there after school everyday until visiting hours were over. Jay knew that Diana was busy with her father. He gave her the space she needed to be with him.

School was a breeze for Diana and she continued to be involved in everything going on there. Diana kept busy. One afternoon when school was over Diana went straight to the hospital to see her father and the Administrator told her that her father was released and had gone home. But where was home? Diana had not found out where he wanted to go after he was released. Diana ran to tell her mother, but her mother already knew. Diana's father had left her mother and her again.

Diana was feeling sad and she went for a walk. She ended up at Jay's house talking to his mother. Jay's mother was so good to Diana all the time. She felt comfortable talking to her.

While Diana was there Jay came in and Diana told him what happened. Jay made a few phone calls and then told Diana that they could talk the rest of the night. Diana thanked him for being a friend. Diana had always told him of the pain of her father's leaving and he helped her forget the pain. That night Jay asked Diana to marry him and said that he would never leave her. He knew what this could do to her loosing her father again. Diana said no but thanked him for caring. I love you so much that I wanted to scream "Yes" as loud as I can but it would not be right for me to used this situation as an excuse to get you all to myself. I would later feel guilty and you would too. We love each other enough to wait until the time is right. Jay said "I am ready baby, and when every you are, I will be here." She asked Jay to take her home so that she could try to go to sleep. Jay said, "Please spend the night with me and let me put you to sleep." Diana remembered how good Jay could make her feel when they made love and said "Yes." They went to his room and Jay undressed Diana and put her in bed. He kissed her and said "I love you baby." They made love and talked all night.

The next day Diana and Jay spent the whole day together and Jay told Diana that he needed her to love him. Diana said, I love you so much Jay. Please don't ever leave me." Jay said, "I could never leave you." Jay took Diana home that night. When Diana got there her mother told her that her father was in Tennessee with his sister and mother and that he was alright. Diana said "Good," and went to say good night to Jay.

Diana's mother asked her if she had slept with Jay last night and Diana said yes. Her mother asked her if she was having sex with him. Diana said yes. Diana told her how much she and Jay loved each other. Her mother told her that she thought what her father and her had was love too, but it wasn't. She said that it was to soon to make the decisions of commitment for both Jay and her. Her mother told her that someday he was going to leave her too. She told Diana that men only think they love you and then they get tired. She said I trusted Jay and his mother to take care of you and he was only thinking of one thing. How could his mother have let this go on?" She asked Diana, "How could you betray my trust like this?" "You are not old enough to have sex!" Diana told her mother that she was responsible and that she knew Jay loved her. Diana's mother said "what are you doing for protection against getting pregnant?" Diana said, "Jay took me to get some birth control pills from the clinic and he had a doctor give me a check-up at the hospital." Diana said, "Mother he really loves me."

Diana's mother called Jay and he said that he would be right over. When Jay got there she told him how she did not want him to see Diana anymore and that she trusted him and he used her daughter to betray her. Jay told her that he loved Diana and that making love to her was just another way of showing her. He said that he would always be here to take care of her. He said Diana is my life and always will be. If you don't believe me now you will.

Diana then came to sit by Jay and he held her hand and said "I love you." Diana's mother said "This is not what I wanted for my daughter, I never could have imagined it, but if you are happy Diana I pray that this doesn't come back to hurt you."

Diana said, " love you mom, and I love Jay and I have to follow my heart." Diana's mother went upstairs to go to bed. Diana and Jay talked about it for a while and then they said good night.

It was the end of the school year and Diana was tired from all she had been through with getting to know her father. Diana spent the summer with her grandparents in Louisiana. Jay took Diana to National Airport and waited with her until her plane started to board. He tried to talk Diana out of leaving. He said that he loved her and needed her. Diana told Jay that the time would pass quickly and that she would love him even more when she returned. They kissed for ten minutes and held each other twice as long. Then Diana was gone. Jay was sad, even minutes after she left he missed her very much. But, Jay was busy running his business so he didn't call or write her.

Diana was sad at first, but she made the best of her summer. While in Louisiana Diana spent a lot of time walking, thinking, and breathing the fresh air. She thought about Jay so much that she couldn't wait to get back to him.

Diana's family was glad to have her visiting them. They went out shopping and visiting friends the whole summer. Diana had a cousin name Melvina that was her favorite cousin and best friend. They went out shopping and visiting friends the whole summer. Diana loved being with them also. Then it was time for her to go home. The summer seemed to have gone by in a few days. When Diana returned she called Jay and he was not there so she talked to his mother. Diana had gifts and wanted to bring them by but she didn't want to surprise Jay if he had someone else there.

Junior's mother told Diana that he would not be back until tomorrow so Diana said that she would come right over. When Diana got there she was glad to see Jay's parents and then she gave them their gifts, kissed them, and went to leave Jay's gift in his room. Diana saw her pictures all over his room and her hair brush still in place along with her sleep shirt. Her tooth brush was still there with her earring's and bracelet in place. Diana knew then that Jay still loved her.

When Diana came out into the living room she asked Jay's father if she could talk to his wife for a minute and he said I'll be in the room. Diana hugged him and said "Thank you." Jay's mother was sitting on the couch waiting to hear what Diana had to say. Diana told her about the talk she and Jay had with her mother about them having sex. Diana explained to her how she and Jay felt about each other and that she wanted her to hear it from her that she and Jay had been having sex. Jay's mother said thank you for wanting to talk to me but I already knew. I could see it in the different ways you looked at each other. I could see that you two had taken your love to that point. I love you as if you were my own daughter and I would never let anyone hurt you. I also, know how much Jay love's you and I trust him. I am glad that you were honest with your mother and I know that she will come around to understanding. Diana hugged her again and said "What would I have done in life without you?" Then she went home and went to sleep.

The next day Jay called her and asked her to come over to his house and Diana said, "No." He said he loved and missed her with all his heart. Diana said, "Good-by Jay." Diana knew that it was time to rescue Jay from the drug scene. She hoped that he would choose her over the drug money. It was time to test the strength of their love. Diana knew that Jay loved her and would do anything for her and she was going to show him that she would never accept him dealing in any kind of drugs.

59

PROM NIGHT

It was the beginning of the last year of high school. Diana
was in school early on the first day. When Jay got there she said
that they could talk after school. Jay saw that Diana had cut her
hair again. He walked up to her kissed her and said, "Baby I missed
you," then he added "What have you done to your hair? Baby
please don't cut your hair again." Jay only needed two credits to
graduate, so he was only scheduled to three classes and he was out
of school by ten o'clock AM. Diana knew he would be leaving
and hoped not to see him much. She loved him so much she was
willing to take the chance of loosing him.

Later when Jay came to pick Diana up from school, they
talked. Diana complained to Jay that selling drugs was wrong. She
said "The same drugs you sell kill the people who struggled for
freedom in this racist country. The white men that produce and
transport this poison are the same white men that kept our race in
slavery for so many years. Less than one hundred years ago, many
white men and women considered our race to be less than human.
Racism today is successful because the white man controls the
black man's thinking. The drugs are a substitute for the chains that
they brought our ancestors over in. The white man is smart enough
to change with the times without changing his mind. The white
man knows that in this day and time he can't practice slavery the
way he did eighty years ago, so he devised another method and that
method is divide, destroy, and control by administering the illegal
drugs." Jay was being educated by Diana in more ways than one.
He began to think the way Diana was preaching. He supported her
in working to warn students about the danger of drugs. Jay was
changing his outlook on selling drugs. He had put a lot of time and
effort in his business but he knew it was time for a change.

Jay started to buy real estate and then he bought a advertising company that was going out of business. Jay was slowly preparing to stop selling drugs.

Meanwhile Diana was valedictorian and homecoming queen. With a 4.0 average, she had offers to more than ten colleges. She along with a hand picked committee organized and planned the whole senior year. She led the year book committee, planned the prom, and wrote the farewell speech for graduation day. She was so busy she did not see that Jay was changing and cleaning up his street ties. He had made so much money for the drug lords that they had become close friends. That made his transition smooth and safe. As a friend they knew that Jay would never turn them in. Jay made it clear that he was finished with the business and that he wanted no contact with them. Jay left the business with no ties.

The end of the school year was coming and Diana was planning for college. Junior was picking Diana up every evening and taking her to his house so that they could spend time together. He shared his new business with her and together they drew up a business plan. Jay took the plan and made the company into a money profit business. He received new and old contracts. He bought more people in on staff and for a while the company was running itself.

Diana's senior year sped by. The teachers and administrators were sad that she was leaving. Diana was wise, smart, and eager to learn and would teach like no other student they had ever met. The principal used to say that "Diana was an angel from heaven."

The week of the prom night Diana told Junior that after graduation she was not going to see him anymore. Jay said that he would never let her go and she could forget that. Diana was sure and persistent and left it at that. Diana refused to see Jay for three days. It was prom night and Diana was so beautiful that Cinderella at the ball would have looked like a maid compared to her. The whole prom admired her and was amazed that Diana could be that pretty. Her dress was from LA. and her shoes were from Connecticut Avenue. Her Hair was all combed to one side and her faced was as smooth as baby skin.

Jay could not stop telling Diana how gorgeous she was. Dancing to the Temptation's "Old Girl," he was thinking of how he could not wait to make love to her. Jay had rented the penthouse at the Marriott on Fourteenth Street, N.W. Diana was ready to go after dancing all night and Jay didn't tell her where they were going until he started driving. Diana said, "I am tired. Please let's just go to sleep when we get there."

When they got there the room was so beautiful that Diana was amazed. Jay carried Diana in the room and sat her on the bed then he sat beside her. He then stretched out his arms motioning for Diana to come and sit on his lap and she did. He started kissing her and she remembered how much she loved him and how good he was at making love to her. Diana and Jay made love until the sun came up and they talked the next day, eating only the basket of fruit left in the room with compliments of the hotel. They started to make love again the next night until the sun came up again. Then Diana told him that she had to go home. Jay asked Diana to stay one more night and she refused.

Jay took Diana home and asked if he could stay for a while. Diana said, "Jay we need to talk." She told him that she needed to go on with her life without him. She said, "If you cared anything about me you would leave me alone. We have had some really good times together and I will never forget them. I don't think that I will ever love anyone as much as I love you. It will take a long time to stop loving you but I know now that I have to stop. The drugs and the kind of life you are living are not for me. I want to go on without having any guilt of what could or will happen in the drug world. It would be compromising too much to sit back and watch you go on. As much as I love you today, and have since I first saw you, I can't and will not support you anymore. Please, Jay, leave and go on without me. " Diana could not stop the tears from falling from her eyes. She got up went to the door, her voice was steady. "Jay thank you for everything, Good-by." Jay walked over to Diana and wiped her face with his hands, looking into her eyes. He said, "Diana I love you more than life itself. I could never leave you for good. I have no life without you. I'm going to love you for the rest of my life. You are so beautiful. I need you in order to go on breathing. I will take care of you for the rest of your life. I am committed to our relationship. I don't know any other way. You are my life. Get some rest and we will talk later. I love you baby." Then he kissed Diana and walked back to his car.

For the next five days Diana and Jay had no communication with each other. Jay was busy closing up his drug deals on the streets and changing his image. He changed his wardrobe from jeans to suits, and traded his red sports car in for a green Mercedes. He spent three days shopping and changing his style.

After being away from Diana for five days, Jay could not take it any more. It was two o'clock one Thursday afternoon when Jay knocked on Diana's door. When Diana answered Jay had a dozen of roses and a box of chocolate candy. Diana was surprised to see him and said "Jay, please come in. Thank you for the flowers, I needed them. And Jay, I needed to see you too." Jay kissed her and said "I love you baby." Jay was dressed in a black suit with a beautiful tie and shined shoes. He looked so good that Diana did not want him to stop holding her. Jay did very little talking and just held her.

When Jay started to tell Diana that he was finished with drugs and that he was going to run his own business she said "Thank you." Jay I love you so much." Jay did not have to say that he had done it for her because she knew it. They talked for three hours about his plans. Diana gave advice where she could. Some friends of Diana's and her mother knocked at the door and they talked for a while and the Diana's mother asked Jay to go to the liquor store to buy some beer and liquor. Jay and one of Diana's cousins went. When they got back Diana's cousin was telling Diana how the girls were after Jay and falling at his feet. Jay kissed her and said they could never compete with you. Diana was happy to hear Jay say that. Jay held Diana all night and they kissed every five minutes. Everyone there could see they were in love.

Diana was scheduled to attend Howard University in September. Jay was in the process of operating his own advertising company. He had bought and sold a variety of real estate in the metro area. Jay was well known in the neighborhood and families that were about to be evicted and put out on the streets would come to him to get their rent money. Jay would always help the families that came to him. He realized that it was their money that made him what he was. If not their money directly, then, from one of their family members. The little kids on the street would always look for money or gifts from Jay. He would give block parties and have famous entertainers there. He would pay for all the food and games. Jay had contact with people of all walks of life because of his million dollar drug business.

Diana was so pleased to know that Jay was giving some of his earnings back to the neighborhood. He never stopped giving back and he was loved by everyone in the neighborhood. Jay left the drug business saying good-by to all contacts, leaving on good terms. He had made money in the drug business and capitalized on it. He put some of the money back into the neighborhood and the rest into a growing business that was his own. Diana could not share this new life with him yet, since she was going to college. They were both traveling in different directions. Their love was being tested again.

HOWARD UNIVERSITY

On the first day of college Junior came to Diana's house early that morning. He wanted to take her to school. Even though Diana told him not to come over, he did. Diana got dressed and he took her to school. Jay told Diana on the way to Howard that he loved her and he was starting a company for her so that when they got married he could take care of her. That meant a lot to Diana. Jay continued to take Diana to school and pick her up after school. The students knew Jay as well as they knew Diana up at Howard. They were known as a couple. Jay would take Diana shopping once a week. He bought all of her clothes. She was the best dressed student at Howard. Jay and Diana spent a lot of time together. Diana would go to his house every day after school and he would listen to her read and do her homework. Jay was becoming familiar with his new business while Diana was in school.

During the summer after Diana's first year at Howard Jay took her on a two weeks vacation to the Caribbean. The cruise would be their most memorable trip together. Jay traveled a lot to different places without Diana during the school year. During the summer months Diana always went with him. Diana spent all of her free time with Jay, and she loved it. Jay love her and he treated her like a princess. He showered her with gifts and let everyone around know that he loved her. But he never gave up his habit of having other women.

All of Jay's women knew about Diana but she didn't know about them. It was the beginning of Diana's second year at Howard and she took on more classes. Jay was busy at work too. He had his longtime friend and mentor, the father of his old girlfriend Veny to be the second in command at his new company. Jay also gave Veny a job. He had started to buy other companies and incorporated them into his. His company had grown to three

million dollars in assets after the second year. Diana and Jay spent
most evenings together and apart most days.

Diana was in Jay's room one day when the phone rang and
Veny called and asked for Jay. Diana said that he was at the store
and he would be right back. Veny said that she would see him at
work tomorrow. Diana was shocked. Jay didn't tell her that he had
given Veny a job. Veny was so in love with Jay that she lived to
come between him and Diana.

When Jay got back Diana told him that Veny had called.
Jay said I was going to tell you tonight. Diana asked, "How long
has she been there?" Jay said, "Two weeks." Diana said, "When
were you going to tell me?" Jay said, "Baby, I love you and I only
want you. You never have to worry about any other girl no matter
where she is. I did it for her father." Diana, to Jay's surprise, said,
"Okay Jay."

In the weeks to come Veny would call five times a week
asking for Jay. Diana picked up the phone one day and told her
that Jay was off from work and when he was not working he did
not converse with his employees. Veny said, "Is that what he tells
you?" We have lunch a lot and we talk after work." Diana hung
up.

When Jay came in the room Diana said, "Jay, look, if there
is something going on with you and Veny tell me now because I'm
tired of her calling here every day. Let her know that I don't want
her calling you after working hours." Jay smiled and said, "Okay,
baby. I love you, too." Diana said, "I mean it, Jay." He kissed her
and said "I love you."

Jay had started going out Friday nights with his friends and
leaving Diana home. She did not mind because she usually had
homework to complete. Jay met a girl name Evelyn that he was
sleeping with on a regular basis when he got away from Diana. The
girl called Jay one day and said that she was pregnant. Jay hung up

on her after saying it was not his. Evelyn called back and talked to Diana telling her about all their meetings. By this time Diana was tired of all the phone calls and notes on Jay's car and people looking at her as if she were deformed.

She told Jay to take her home one night and on the way she told him she knew about Evelyn being pregnant. He said "The baby is not mine." Diana said, "Did you sleep with her?" and he did not answer. Diana asked Jay to leave her alone and she said "I never want to see you again. Please take care of your baby. I can't accept you with a baby." Jay pleaded and begged Diana to believe that it was not his. As they were getting out of the car at Diana's house Evelyn was in front of Diana's asking Jay could she talk to him. Diana said, "Please go." Jay walked over and scolded the girl. He said ,"I will never claim that baby and I will never want you. What you have done to Diana is unforgivable. He told her never to call him again." He then went up stairs to Diana's house. Diana asked Jay to leave and never come back. Jay was so hurt he just left.

Diana went to sleep trying not to think about the girl or Jay. Jay called Diana but she unplugged the phone. Two weeks later Jay went up to Howard to see Diana and asked her to let him take her to dinner so they could talk. Diana had missed Jay and wanted to see him. She said, "Okay." Jay picked her up and took her to dinner at Hogates on the Waterfront. He explained that the girl was trying to trap him and that he was going to get out of this. He asked Diana to give him some time. She said, "Jay "It's over. Let's just be friends." Jay said, "I love you and I miss you. I need to hold you and feel you. I don't need a friend." Diana said, " Jay, I'm tired of the other women that you need in your life. I can't take it anymore. Please let's just end this." Diana asked Jay to take her home.

When they pulled up in front of Diana's apartment building Evelyn was there again. This time when she called Jay he did not go. Then Evelyn called Diana. Diana went so Jay went behind her. Evelyn told Diana "I'm sorry for the trouble I have caused. Jay did not get me pregnant. I was already pregnant when we were together, I knew that he could afford to take care of my baby so I wanted to blame him. I was wrong and I hope you two can forgive me. I'm sorry." Diana said, "Thank you," and went up the stairs, and Jay went behind her. Jay said, Diana, I'm sorry." Diana said, "Baby, I love you so much. Why do you continue to hurt me?" He held her and said "I don't know. All I know is that I love you very much and I don't want to loose you." Diana kissed him. Jay asked Diana to come with him that night and Diana said, "No," but I will come and spend the weekend with you. I love you baby." Jay went home a happy man that night.

Diana finished her second year at Howard with a 4.0 average. During the summer months she and Jay spent all their time together. Jay had some cousins coming from out of town and Diana was going to come over to meet them the next day. Jay's mother always introduced Diana as her daughter, so they were expecting to see Diana as Jay's sister, not as his girlfriend. One of Jay's little cousins was teasing him before he went to pick Diana up. The cousin saw Diana's pictures all around and asked Jay how much did he pay the girl for her pictures. Jay laughed and said two hundred dollars. Jay then left to get Diana.

When they got back and Diana walked in, the family was amazed at how beautiful Diana was. She had on blue shorts with the matching top and some silver slippers. Her hair was out and her toes were polished orange. Jay's cousin ran up and said "You did pay her." Diana said Jay "Who did you pay?" and he laughed again. Diana took her bag in the room and came back to meet everyone. Jay was always kissing and hugging Diana and his cousins stared. They weren't familiar with this kind of love. Jay's aunt said "Jay, do you see other girls?" and Jay asked, "Are there other girls in this world?" Diana smiled happily. Jay's little cousin aunt said "Jay, do you see other girls?" and Jay asked, "Are there other girls in this world?" Diana smiled happily. Jay's little cousin came up to Diana and said you are even prettier than your pictures. Diana said thank you.

They all sat around talking and Diana got tired and said good night and went to Jay's room. Jay spent some time with his cousins and when he got to bed Diana was asleep. He kissed her and said good night. The next day the family went to King's Dominion. Jay and Diana rode on all the rides, and Jay won Diana stuffed animals and they took more pictures. Diana loved being in the park. On the way home Diana asked Jay to stop the car and he did. Diana got out and asked Jay to get out and he did. She said, "Baby I need you to hold me. I love you so much and I am so glad that you chose me." "Thanks baby," Jay said, "I love you too baby."

For the rest of the summer Jay and Diana spent all their time together. They were so much in love. It was the beginning of Diana's last year at Howard and she was working even harder to maintain her 4.0 average. Veny was not losing anytime either. She was falling more and more in love with Jay. She asked Jay to go out one night and he said no and told her that he loved Diana. Veny then said that she had him first and that he should love her because they grew up together. Jay told her that they never had anything and that he would always love Diana.

Later that night Veny took some pills and tried to kill herself. Jay and Diana was just getting to Jay's house from Howard when Veny's father called. Jay said that he would be right there. She was in Prince George's Hospital. Diana said "Baby, go ahead I'll wait here." Diana waited in Jay's bed for him and when he got there he did not want to talk. It was the next day when he told Diana what had happened. Diana knew then that Veny would spend the rest of her life trying to get Jay.

Diana was still going to school in the day and spending every evening with Jay and most of the nights. At the end of Diana's last year though, she started going home to study and Jay started to go out again, sometimes staying out all night. Diana could not think about that because she was trying to graduate with honors from Howard.

On graduation day Jay and his mother and father were there. Diana's mother and her aunts and cousins were there too. It had been a long, hard struggle but it was worth it. Everyone was so proud of Diana. Her mother had a surprise party for her. Diana's favorite cousin Mel, came up from Louisiana. They partied all night. After Jay left, Diana and her cousin talked until dawn. When Jay called Diana in the morning she told him she had not been to sleep yet. He said that he loved her and that he would see her later. When he did see her, he told her something that would separate them from their love affair for a long time.

BELIEVE IN YOUR DREAMS

One Saturday morning, when Diana got up and called Jay and he was not home. Diana waited all day and did not hear from Jay. That night Jay knocked at Diana's door. She was so glad to see him that she just kissed and held him for a long time. When Diana did speak she said, "Jay, where have you been? I have been worried to death. Why didn't you call me?" Jay said, "Sit down, Diana. I have something to tell you." Diana sat down, seeing in Jay's eyes that something was wrong.

Jay started off by telling Diana how much he loved her. Diana wanted to know what was going on. "Jay, what is wrong?" He didn't want to tell her, but he did. He answered. " I've been in jail." Diana couldn't believe what she was hearing. He went on to say, "I was arrested for rape and spent the whole day in jail. " Diana said "Rape! Who?" "Cynthia Tate." "When did you do this?" Jay said "Baby, if you never believe me again, please believe that I never raped anyone in my life. She is angry because I won't see her anymore and this is her way of punishing me." "Did you sleep with her?" Diana asked. "Yes." Jay said. "How many times?" Diana asked. "I don't' remember." He said. Then Diana realizing how unfaithful Jay had been asked, "But it was more than twice." Jay said "Yes." Diana started to cry. "Why?" "I don't know, we were separated and I was feeling sorry for myself. I'm sorry Diana." "Sorry doesn't stop the hurt," Jay told Diana that he had to meet with his lawyer on Monday. Diana asked Jay to leave: She said she needed to lie down before she passed out. Jay said that he would wait downstairs until she got up. Diana said, "No, please leave. I'll call you later."

Diana cried for two whole days. On Monday morning
Diana called Jay and told him that she would be thinking of him and
praying for him. Jay told her that he would be over as soon as he
left the lawyer. Diana was trying to be supportive even though she
was hurting. When Jay got there he asked Diana to come with him
so they could talk. Diana agreed.

As they were driving over to Jay's house he told her that
there was going to be a trial. He asked Diana if she would be there
for him. Jay said the only way he would have the strength to fight
back would be with Diana beside him. Diana said, "I will be by
your side through this trial." Diana was waiting to tell Jay later that
after this she was leaving him for good.

Diana went with Jay to the lawyer's office for meetings.
She met with the District Attorney with him and his lawyer. The
DA. liked Diana and thought that Jay was crazy for hurting her the
way he had and that he should be taken out of Diana's life. But
Diana and Jay had a lot of history together and they had gone
through so much. They stood in the mist of many storms before
this one and came out together.

The first court date was set. Diana sat right behind Jay in
the courtroom and when things got tough she reached out and held
his hand. Diana listened for weeks to witnesses telling about
meeting's between Jay and Cynthia. She saw an endless parade of
friends who had seen them together. By this time Diana was
starting to get sick from hearing all the deceitful things Jay had
done. The trial was ending and Cynthia had to tell her part. Diana
was listening to her about a sexual relationship between her and
Jay. She got so dizzy that she ran out of the courtroom. The bailiff
went behind her. Jay tried to go but his lawyer asked him not to
move. Jay sent his father out to take Diana home. Diana was out

in front of the court and when Jay's father got there she had calmed down. Jay's father offered to take her home but Diana said she wanted to wait for Jay. When Jay walked out he took Diana's hand and they went to his car. Jay tried to tell Diana that he was sorry. Diana told Jay to take her home, and he did. Jay asked if he could stay the night and Diana refused. "When this is all over, Jay, I will be through with you. I will support you through this and then it will be over. Good-by, Jay." Diana turned and walked up her steps. She was so hurt that Jay could see it in her walk. Diana cried herself to sleep one more night.

The next morning when Jay picked Diana up they drove to the court where they met Cynthia on the court steps. Diana and Jay tried to walk by but Cynthia wanted to talk. Diana asked her why was she doing this. Diana said, "You and I both know that Jay would never have to rape any one, and that he could just snap his finger and have any women he wanted. If it's to let me know that he cheated on me, then I know, so you can end this lie. I love Jay and we will spend the rest of our lives together no matter what happens. Please stop this now before you hurt yourself anymore."

Cynthia was surprised and almost looked as if she was sorry. Jay was surprised too. He knew Diana was leaving him after the trial. As they walked off Diana looked at him and said, "Everything I told Cynthia was what I believed for a long time. But when this trial is over I don't ever want to see you again."

Jay walked in court sad. He had lost the one person he loved most in the world. But he didn't have time to imagine life without Diana. The trial was ending. The judge was just about to render a verdict when Cynthia stood up and said, "I made a mistake. I was not raped. I was hurt and I wanted to hurt him. I wanted him to return my love. I know now that he could never do that. I also know why. I am sorry."

The DA dropped the charges and the judge threw the case out of court. He recommended that Cynthia get psychiatric help, and she agreed. Diana and Jay walked to Jay's car. On the way they ran into the DA. who told Diana that he was glad that this was over for her sake. He gave her a business card and asked her to call if she needed anything. Jay stood there and the DA. looked at him and Jay looked at him then walked away.

Diana was quiet on the way home. Jay tried to get Diana to give him another chance but she said no. Diana told Jay that she could never trust him again. She said "Too much has happened. Let's leave it alone, please." Jay protested, "I'll always love you and I will never stop trying to get you."

The next four days Diana tried to keep busy, not staying home or unplugging the phone so Jay could not reach her. On the fifth day Jay called Diana on her mother's phone and told her that it was his parents anniversary again and that they would be disappointed if she didn't show up at their anniversary dinner. Jay said that he was giving them a surprise party afterwards. He asked Diana to go and then come to his house to meet the people who would already be there waiting to surprise his parents. Diana agreed and told Jay to pick her up. Jay was so happy that he forgot to tell Diana what time. He called her back and told her that he would pick her up at six o'clock that evening.

Diana wore a Jade green dress with her birthstone necklace and bracelet that Jay had given her many years ago. She was beautiful. Jay could not keep his eyes off of her. The dinner was nice and Jay's parents enjoyed Diana's company and the meal. Jay talked to Diana about what was going to happen after they got back home. He told her all about the surprise party plan. He never stopped looking at her.

After dinner they went back to Jay's parent's house. When they opened the door all their friend and family yelled "surprise!" Jay's mother kissed him and Diana and thanked them both.

When They got to the house Diana went to his room to check her hair and Jay followed. He said "You are so pretty. Please let me look at you in here for as long as I can." Diana said, "Please Jay. This night is for your parents, because I love them." Jay asked "Do you still love me?" Diana walked out the room without answering. As Diana was walking out of Jay's room his mother took Diana in the room and talked to her. She said, "Dee, I know you are here for us, I want to thank you and let you know that you will always be my daughter no matter what happens with you and Jay. I miss you so much, please try to come and see me while Jay is at work." Diana said, answering her sincerely, "I love you too and I will." Jay came in just then. "Is this a private party?" He joked. Diana said, "No."

They all walked out into the living room, where Jay's cousin was gathering everyone to take family pictures. Jay got a chance to hold Diana as they were posing for pictures and he enjoyed every precious second.

Later Diana asked Jay to take her home. "Please stay, " Jay begged. Diana was firm "Jay, please take me home." Jay said "Yes." They left and when Diana got home she thanked Jay again and said good-by. Jay said, "You don't have to thank me. I love you."

In the days that followed Diana never plugged in her phone so Jay could not call. Diana would go to see Jay's mother during the day and spend the entire afternoon with her. One day Jay came home early and Diana was there. He was glad to see Diana and did not want her to go. He asked if they could talk and Diana said, "No, and that her mother was on the way to pick her up.' Jay asked to take her home. Diana said "No." Jay's mother watched them as they talked hoping they could get back together. Diana walked over and kissed her good-by.

He had started stopping by Diana's house every evening after work. Diana and her friends and cousins were playing cards in the kitchen one evening when he came by. The older people were in the living room with Diana's mother and boyfriend. Jay would always come over to go to the liquor store for them.

Three months passed and Jay was still watching Diana from a distance. He couldn't touch her or kiss her. It was difficult for Jay not to be able to be there with Diana. One evening Jay came in and Diana's mother asked him to go to the store for her and he agreed. Jay asked Diana if she would go with him and Diana turned him down.

Jay then asked "Could I see you upstairs for a minute?" Diana didn't even look at him and said, "I'm talking right now." "Diana, come here, "In a demanding voice. Diana didn't want Jay to make a scene so she agreed to go upstairs with him.

When they got to the top of the stairs, Jay pulled Diana into her room and said, "Look, Diana I know you think what we had is over. I'm trying to live with that. But don't expect me to be in the same room with you and not touch you or not sit by you. Please don't ask me to pretend we were never friends." Diana's voice was soft, "If you don't want to see me from a distance, then don't come over here. "Jay's answer was swift and sure. "Diana I love you and I can't hold myself back from touching you or saying hello when I see you. Don't ever let me walk into a room again without acknowledging me." Diana said, "Jay, please! What do you want from me? Please leave me alone." Jay persisted, "Diana I can't do that, just like that. It takes time to stop loving someone as much as I love you." Diana wanted to get out of the room with Jay so she said Okay, Jay, I will sit by you and acknowledge you to make you comfortable. Please let me out of here." Diana went back downstairs and Jay followed. He asked Diana if she wanted anything and she said "No thank you."

When Jay returned, Diana and her friends were playing spades in the kitchen and Jay put the beer in the ice box and went into the living room. When the girls finished, they joined the other's in the living room and Diana went to sit by Jay. His smile showed his happiness. When everyone left. Jay asked Diana if she still loved him and Diana said "Jay, good night. I am tired." Jay then said that he loved her and missed her and then he left.

The next week it started to snow again and Diana's mother had to go to Atlanta, Georgia for training on her job for two weeks. Jay came by and stayed with Diana until late at night for the first two days. They talked about the day and Jay's job and watched TV. After the second night Jay asked Diana to come and stay at his house but she said, "No. On the third day, when Jay got to Diana's he told her that he had to go to New York for three days and that he didn't want to leave her alone in her apartment. Earlier Jay's mother had called and asked Diana to come and stay there for a while. Diana told Jay she would come, but when he got back she was coming home. Jay agreed. Diana packed a few things and then left. Jay was also leaving that night.

When they arrived at Jay's house, Diana went to his room to put her bag and then came back out to ask Jay what time his flight was leaving and he said nine o'clock. It was four o'clock at that time. Jay's mother had fixed dinner and they all sat down to eat.

Everyone was happy that Diana was there. Jay walked into the living room after dinner and started to light a fire. Diana helped clean the kitchen and went into the living room where Jay and his father were. Diana said "Jay, are you already packed?" He said, "Yes, my bags are in the car." Jay walked over to Diana and spoke tenderly saying "Thank you for being here, I can go in peace now. I would have worried so much about you. Diana thanked him. Jay said, "I love you. You are so beautiful. I'll miss you." Jay talked for a while with Diana about his meeting in New York and then it was time to go. As Jay said "Good-by and walked out the door Diana ran behind him. When she reached him she said, "Jay!" and then he kissed her. After kissing him back she said "Jay, please be careful. I love you and I want you to come back to be with me." Jay and Diana had a saying that they would say in times when their relationship was troubled (If we are with each other we can work it out) Diana said that to Jay as he walked her back into the house and kissed her again. He said good-by to his mother and father and left. Shortly after that Diana went to Jay's room to go to bed.

At about one o'clock A.M. Jay called. Diana answered the phone. "Jay, are you just getting there? "Yes" Jay told her the snow was bad and that the plane was delayed. Jay asked Diana what she was wearing and Diana told him his pajama shirt. He said that he could see her and that he never wanted to sleep in that room again. He wanted it to be hers. He said as long as she was there he could picture her there and be happy. Diana said, "Good night, Jay. Call back tomorrow." He said, "I love you baby" and hung up.

Diana couldn't go back to sleep after Jay's call. She loved Jay too but she couldn't tell him because she was trying not to love him. The next morning Jay's father got a call that his brother was sick in Baltimore and that they should get there before the snow got too bad. They asked Diana to come with them and she said no, that she would be okay. They left and said they would be back tomorrow. Diana locked up and went to Jay's room. Jay called and told Diana that he was going to try to get back soon. He asked her if she wanted him to leave now and she said no, I'll be okay. Jay said that he would call back later. In the meantime it had started to snow really badly. There was five feet of snow on the ground and it was still snowing. Diana started to get a little worried because she had not heard from Jay and it was nine o'clock at night. Jay's parents called every four hours to check on Diana. She took her bath and went to bed.

When Diana woke up Jay was sitting in the chair watching over her. She was so glad to see him "Jay! (reaching to hug him) how long have you been there?" she asked. "About three hours", he said. Diana was puzzled, "How did you get out of New York? Are planes flying?" Jay said no, I hired a private plane." "Thank God you are alright!," Diana exulted. Jay's voice was deep and reassuring. "Go back to sleep, baby. I'll take care of you." Diana wanting to hold Jay forever said, "Jay aren't you tired?" Jay said "No, I'm getting use to not sleeping. "Jay went into the living room to start a fire. As the wood began to crackle, Diana began to feel safe, and she fell sound asleep. When Diana woke up Jay was on the couch asleep and Diana woke him up. "Baby, come to bed," she whispered. He said, "Okay." Jay undressed to go to bed and Diana dressed to start breakfast. Diana fixed Jay breakfast in bed and he ate every bit, praising her cooking throughout the meal." They talked all the next day and watched TV together. Jay's mother called and said they were going to stay for a while longer since Jay was back.

Jay had a friend who was giving a party and asked Jay if they would come. Jay asked Diana if they could go and she said okay. They got dressed and went to the party. The snow had started to melt. Jay danced and held Diana the whole night. They laughed and talked until the party was over.

On the way home from the party Diana told Jay that she had forgotten how much fun they used to have together. Jay said, "I had a good time too." "Thank you, baby." Diana echoed his joy. Thank you, Jay for asking me to come. They got home and Jay asked Diana if she was hungry and she said "No." He then asked "Do you want to watch TV. " Diana said "Yes." Jay started a fire and Diana and Jay sat on the couch and watched TV. Diana started to get sleepy and laid on the couch with her head on Jay's lap. He rubbed her head and her hair until she went to sleep and he watched her. When she woke up and Jay told her to go to bed. Diana said, "Will you come with me?" Jay was shocked, but he said "Yes." Diana undressed and got in bed while Jay put the fire out. When Jay came in, Diana asked him to turn the music on and he did. After Jay undressed and got in bed Diana looked at him and said "Jay, I love you." Jay had wanted to hear Diana say these words for so long. Diana turned over and got on top of Jay and kissed him. Jay told Diana that he loved her and he had waited so long for this moment. Diana told Jay that she was scared and he said, "I'll help you." And he rolled Diana over and made love to her until the sun came up.

Diana and Jay did not get out of bed for two days. They loved each other and they had found their hearts again. Diana told Jay she loved him and went to sleep. When she woke up Jay was in the living room talking to his parents. Diana went in the room to say hello and to tell them that she had missed them. Jay walked over and kissed her and said he loved her. Later Diana's mother called and asked her to come home. Jay didn't want Diana to leave. But Diana said she had to go but she would come back for the weekend.

Jay took Diana home that night, and stayed until three o'clock AM. He had to go to work the next day, but after work he went straight to Diana's to see her. When he came in at first Diana didn't see him. When she did see him she ran to kiss him, and told him that she missed him. Jay told Diana that he could not sleep without her and that he had to have her with him. Diana said "Jay, we have the weekend." For months Diana and Jay spent every waken moment together or on the phone with each other. They were falling more and more deeply in love.

In may Jay had to go to Chicago for a meeting and he asked Diana to go with him. Diana said yes, but, she added that she couldn't leave on Monday. She had a doctor's appointment on Tuesday that she could not miss. She said that she would meet him there on Tuesday. Jay agreed. The Monday that Jay left Diana missed him so much. Jay had spent every night with her until she fell to sleep.

Tuesday Diana left for Chicago. When she arrived at O'Hare Airport Jay had the hotel limo waiting for her. When the limo left O'Hare Airport for downtown Chicago Diana watched the scenes flash by her window. When she got to the hotel Jay was in the lobby with two business associates. Diana walked in and the men started pouring over her. When Jay looked up he saw it was Diana. They ran to hug each other and then walked to the elevator that went to their room on the eighteenth floor. Jay had a two bedroom suite with a foyer and a sitting room before the bedrooms. He ordered a basket of fruit and a bottle of champagne bought up. Diana and Jay put the Do Not Disturb sign on the door and went to bed. They made love all night long.

Jay went to his meeting the next day and then he took Diana to dinner that night and then the limo rode them around downtown Chicago. On Thursday Jay told Diana that he had bought her a ticket to the Oprah Winfrey show. Diana was so excited that she did not hear Jay say that Oprah was a business associate.

Jay had the limo take Diana to the show. She wore a red suit with Italian pumps to match. Oprah welcomed Diana and said that she was expecting her.

When Diana got back to the hotel room Jay was there waiting for her. She told him that she had met Oprah and that they had talked. Jay said, "I know, she called and asked us to join her and Stedman for dinner. " Diana couldn't believe the good news. She thanked Jay and kissed him. Between kissing she managed to say "Jay what will I wear?" His answer thrilled her. "I had some gowns bought over for you to look at, and when you are ready they will come up and show them." Diana said "Jay, how can I ever thank you enough," and he smiled as he always did when she was happy. Diana picked a silver gown with some gold and silver pumps. She looked beautiful.

They arrived at eight o'clock sharp. Oprah opened the door and welcomed them in. Her apartment was so gorgeous it looked like a museum. Stedman was better looking in person, and he was a gentleman. Dinner went well and afterwards they said their good-by's and left for the hotel. When Diana got to the hotel she told Jay that she was the happiest girl in the world and Jay said "Baby, it gets better." The next day after Jay's meeting he took Diana shopping at the river front in downtown Chicago. The next day they left. When they got home Diana was so tired she slept all day. When she woke up Jay was kissing her. He told her that he loved her and never wanted her to sleep away from him again. Diana did not want to leave Jay either. But she knew she could not stay with him. Her grandparents teachings taught against living with a man and not being married. She could not forget their teachings. Her mother wouldn't go for it either. After two months Diana told Jay she had to go home. Jay begged her not to go and he was hurt when she said she had to go. He was hurt all day. Jay took Diana home and stayed with her until early mornings as he so often did when she was home. He did not want to leave Diana and sleep by himself.

The week was long for Jay without Diana at his side. Diana came over for the weekend Friday. She told Jay's mother how happy they were and confided that if Jay ever asked her to marry him again she was going to say yes. Jay's mother knew that Jay was taking Diana to dinner that night to ask her to marry him, she started to plan for a surprise party at her house after they got back from dinner. Jay and Diana left for dinner. They arrived at Houston's in Rockville and was seated. Jay asked Diana to turn her chair out from the table and Diana asked why. Jay said "Just trust me, baby." She moved her chair and he kneeled in front of her . "Baby I love you more than anything in this world and I want you to be my wife. Will you marry me?" Jay opened a box and pulled out a three karat diamond ring and Diana was in tears. She let Jay put the ring on and she said "Baby I would love to marry you. I love you too." They kissed and Diana couldn't stop crying. Jay held her and kissed her. After dinner they went home and when Jay opened the door. Diana's mother said "Surprise!" Diana wondered "How did you know?" Jay's mother answered "I knew Jay was going to ask you to marry him tonight and I knew you were going to say yes." They all hugged and kissed and drank champagne all night.

Diana and Jay against all the odds were going to be together after all. Their love had stood through the storms.

DIANA GOES TO WORK

It was April and Jay's birthday was coming up. Jay's mother was planning a party for Jay with a few friends and family. Diana helped plan the party too. Diana knew the perfect gift for Jay. She would give him a birthday card saying "Jay will you marry me the first Saturday in June of 1985.

It was the day of the party and Jay was enjoying himself talking with friends. He thanked everyone for coming and proceeded to open his gifts. Diana was standing in the back of the room so that the family who doesn't get to see Jay much can spend some time with him. She watched as they brought their gifts forward. Jay finished with most of the gifts when he noticed Diana was not near by. "Where is Diana?" He asked. Diana called out from the other side of the room. "I'm right here baby." He picked up the next card, which was from Diana. When Jay opened the card and read it, he jumped up and went over to Diana and said, "Thank you Baby. I love you." Then he kissed her.

Soon the crowd asked Jay to finish opening the gifts and Jay said, "I have the only gift I have ever wanted." The music started and Jay and Diana danced as if they were the only two people in the room. They told the crowd that they had set a wedding day and everyone congratulated them. Jay's mother was so happy that she couldn't wait to talk to Diana about getting her a dress and shoes for the wedding. She grabbed Diana after Jay turned for a minute and led her to the kitchen. As they were talking Jay came in and told his mother that it was his birthday and that he wanted Diana beside him all night. His mother told him "But we have so much to do in such a short time." Jay said, Mom, you have a whole year and five months." Diana looked at him. "Jay that isn't a long time to plan the biggest wedding in the universe!" Jay said, "I understand, do what ever you want. "Just promise me that on the day of our wedding, you'll be there to marry me." Jay kissed Diana and said, "I love you baby."

Diana had always told Jay that she could not get married until she got a job. She believed that the bride should pay for the wedding, and that if the groom paid, the marriage wouldn't last. Jay told Diana he didn't want her to work. Diana said that she couldn't marry him if she didn't work to pay for the wedding, so Jay agreed. He told Diana that he would help her find a job. That made her very happy.

Diana and Jay looked in the newspaper ads in the Washington Post for a week. They didn't find anything.

Then Jay remembered that he had a friend working for a publishing company on 7th Street, N.W. Jay asked his friend if he could get Diana an interview with the owner. His friend agreed. Diana was more than qualified for the job and impressed the president of the company who hired Diana on the spot.

Terry Bradley the manager that Diana worked for was a female who was envious of Diana's beauty. She was so jealous that she tried to make it as hard as she could for Diana.

Jay took Diana to work in the mornings and picked her up in the evenings. Diana was happy working. Jay was getting used to her working too. One night, Diana asked Jay to take her to dinner so that they could talk and he said "Okay." After dinner Diana told Jay about the hard time she was having with Terry Bradley. Jay assured Diana that things would get better, and added that she could quit any time she wanted to. But Diana was not a quitter.

Jay took Diana home and said that he would see her tomorrow. Diana was wondering why Jay didn't want to stay with her for a while but she didn't question him. She just kissed him good night and went to her room.

Jay went home and called an emergency meeting with his staff. It was nine o'clock and Jay asked everyone to meet him in his office by ten o'clock. Jay's accountant, secretary, managers, and his five lawyers were there when he got there. Jay thanked everyone for coming out on such a short notice. Jay told them that he wanted to buy the publishing company that Diana was working for and that he wanted it in one week. Also, Jay told the attorneys and his public relations manager that he didn't want anyone to know that he owned the company after it was bought. He said that the president of his company could act as liaison. Jay told them that even though Diana now owned half of the company, he did not want her to know yet. Everyone agreed to get started the next day. Jay told them to keep him informed on a daily basis. He thanked them again and said good night.

The days followed Jay tried to make it as comfortable for Diana after work as he could. He was always there to make her feel relaxed and he enjoyed having her with him everyday.

At the end of the week, as Jay had hoped, the owner agreed to meet with representatives from Jay's company. He was losing money and wanted out. Jay wanted the company and he was not going to overpay for it. After a few minor changes in the contracts the company was Jay's and the deal was done. Jay asked his president to go in on Monday and make the necessary personnel changes. He asked him to give Diana a division and to put Terry Bradley under Diana. Using Diana's insights and intelligence Jay was going to bring the company out of debt. He planned to give the company to Diana later.

Terry didn't like the new changes and accused Diana of sleeping with the owner for her position. That was not far from the truth. Even Diana had no idea how true it was and was furious with Terry. When She told Jay what had happened he acted surprised and said he knew that things would work out for her. They celebrated that night over dinner. The days at work were easier for Diana knowing that Terry was not her supervisor, but Terry did not stop harassing Diana. Diana didn't want to suggest firing Terry or moving her although, Terry was hateful, Diana thought if "I just ignore her and let her work, she will learn to become a team member and stop the foolishness." Terry spent the rest of her time with the company
blaming Diana for what ever went wrong. Diana went on making a difference in the company and the results of Diana's hard work soon began to show.

The day had come for Diana to be fitted for her dress. Diana needed one thousand dollars for the dress maker and asked Jay to get it for her out of their bank account. Even though Jay had Diana's name on all of his bank accounts, she used them only for her earned money. Jay would always leave Diana her allowance money in her drawer were he had left it for the last ten years. He always made sure that Diana had three to four hundred dollars a week. Jay paid for everything with his company card and never needed money for himself. He bought all his and Diana's clothes with his company card. He had become a very rich man. Jay was going to have some friends over to watch the basket ball game. After jay gave her the money Diana kissed him good-by and she and Jay's mother left. Jay forgot to ask Diana to call him when she was on her way back so that he could wait for her. So he dialed her on his car phone. "Baby I just left you," Diana said when she picked up the phone and heard Jay's voice. Jay said, "But I already miss you." He told Diana to call when she was on her way back and that he loved her. Diana said "I love you too baby," and hung up.

Diana was very pleased with the dress she picked and the lady was going to make it. She made dresses for such stars as Jacee Haywood, Regina Pryor, Effi Barry, and a host of others. She was as good as her reputation said she was. She was going to make Diana the most beautiful wedding dress in the world. The dress would be made for a princess. And in many ways Diana was a princess to so many people.

Diana went home and tried not to talk much about her dress to Jay. She talked about everything but her dress and Jay said, "Baby, you didn't tell me about your dress." Diana was afraid that Jay would ask. "Jay, I can't. I want you to be surprised and I want to be so beautiful that you never forget that day. Then Jay replied, "Diana I can't imagine you anymore beautiful than you are now."

Diana and Jay were the happiest they had ever been. They had started to plan their future as husband and wife, and they spent almost every minute together.

It was September, one fall day the year 1984. Diana's mother called to tell her that her grandfather was sick and that she should go home as soon as possible. When Diana hung up Jay could see the sad look on her face. He ran over to her and said, "Baby, what's wrong?" Diana answered "Jay, my grandfather is sick and I need to go home." Diana continued saying, "I am needed at work for a business deal that I have been working on for two months. I don't know how to tell them I can't be there." Jay said, "Baby, I'll call my secretary and have her get you and your mother a flight out Friday." It was Thursday. Jay said that he would take care of the deal. Diana told him that he couldn't because he didn't know anything about it. He told her that he would learn from her and take over and then he asked her to trust him. He told Diana to talk to her supervisor and see what he says. Diana did and her supervisor told her to go ahead, saying that he would put the project on hold for however long she needed. Diana thanked him and went to prepare her staff to continue while she was gone.

When Jay picked Diana up that evening she told him that he was right and her supervisor was very understanding. Jay said, I felt he would be. He sounds like a good man." Jay then told Diana that he was going to join her the following Friday. Diana was so happy that she reached over and kissed him so hard the he could not see the cars in front of him, so he hit brakes very hard. They stopped and kissed each other and then drove home.

Diana had to pack and get ready. As Jay watched her, he told Diana how much he was going to miss her. Diana told Jay that if any other girls looked at him to act like he was blind and didn't see them. She told him that she loved him so much she could not live without him. Jay said, "Baby I could never live without you either. I love you, too." It was Friday and Diana was leaving. Jay drove her to the airport. They kissed each other good-by and Diana told Jay she would call him when she got there. Jay watched as the plane took off and went home missing Diana.

Diana enjoyed spending time with her grandparents. She had forgotten how much she loved it there. Everyone came by to see her. There were old friends, and family and even people who had heard about Diana and wanted to meet her. It wasn't until late at night after all the company left that Diana had time to call Jay. Jay missed Diana so much that he decided to join her earlier than a week. After the third day Jay decided to surprise Diana and meet her. He took a flight out to Louisiana.

When Jay drove up in a gold Mercedes looking identical to the one he drove at home everyone looked. There was a crowd on the porch and Diana was in the inside. Jay got out of the car and walked up to the porch and asked if Diana was around. He was always so sure of himself. He had never been there or even in the state of Louisiana before, yet he was able to find the house Diana's grandparent's lived in. Mel, Diana's cousin who had met Jay before came out and said, "Jay what are you doing here?" Jay said,

"Looking for my Baby." Diana thought she heard Jay and went to the door. She ran out when she saw him, holding and kissing him. Diana said, "Baby, I thought you were coming Friday." He told her that he couldn't wait and that he missed her. Diana's grandfather was in his room resting. When Diana took Jay in it was like they had known each other for years. Diana had talked so much about them to each other that they were no strangers. Diana's grandfather liked Jay so much that they talked for hours. Later Diana's cousin husband asked if Jay wanted to go out with the "fellahs" later. Jay asked Diana if it would be okay and she said yes. Diana packed her bags and Jay put them in his rental car trunk.

They went to Jay's hotel suite in downtown New Iberia so Jay could get ready to go out. When Diana got to the hotel Jay had ordered a fruit basket and a bottle of champagne. Diana and Jay put their usual Do Not Disturb sign on the door and made passionate love for hours. Afterwards Diana told Jay that when he went out the girls were going to fall at his feet. She asked him to not sleep with any of them. Jay told Diana that he loved her and she was the only person he wanted to sleep with. Diana kissed him and told him to remember that he loved her. Jay said, "Baby, I live for our love." Jay and Diana went back to her grandfather's and Jay left with the guys. They had two car loads, with Jay driving his rental Mercedes. The guys hung out in a club called Leo's where customers could dance and drink all night. The girls really did throw themselves at Jay just as Diana thought they would. There was one girl there that was very pretty and she like Jay and asked him to dance. Jay danced with the girl and they sat together at tables. The girl's name was Sheila. She asked Jay to go home with her. He told her that he couldn't because his fiancee wouldn't understand. He told her that if he was not involved she would be the girl for him. Jay gave her two hundred dollars and told her to buy her something nice and then thanked her for the night.

When the club closed it was three AM. The guys were drunk when they got back and ready to drink some more. They were sitting around discussing what happened when Diana came over and told Jay she was ready to go. Jay and Diana said good night and left. Diana was quiet on the way to the hotel and Jay thought something was wrong. Jay told Diana what had happened and that he never stopped thinking of her. She smiled and said "I love you baby." When they got home Diana told Jay that she was proud of how he handled that situation with the girl and that she knew it was hard for him. Jay said, "Baby it really wasn't hard. Loving you makes it easy." Diana said, "You know Jay, I want something from you too." Jay said jokingly "Okay! how much do you want?" And he handed her his billfold. She said, " I don't want your money." Jay kissed her and they went to bed.

The next day they hung out all day with Diana's cousins at different family member's houses. Diana showed Jay every place she could think of and told him all about what she did when she was little. That night Diana and Jay went by to tell her grandfather that they would spend the whole day together tomorrow, but when they got there Diana's mother told her that he was sick and that they were going to take him to the hospital the next day. Diana started to cry and Jay held her and kissed her. He told her that her grandfather would be alright. Diana said, "Jay let's leave so that we can be here early tomorrow." Diana's cousins wanted to party again that night but Jay told them that he had to take his baby home. The next day they went to Diana's grandfather's house and took him to the hospital. Diana told Jay that she wanted to stay with him and that he could go. Jay said, I will stay with you as long as you need to be here." Jay held Diana and kissed her. Diana and Jay were the only ones left after the other family members had gone. Diana stayed in the room with her grandfather until morning and Jay waited outside in the waiting room.

The next day when Diana's mother got there she told Jay to take Diana home for a while to get some rest. Jay asked Diana to go with him for a while and promised that he would bring her back later. Diana kissed her mother and said that she would be back soon. Diana and her mother could sense that the end was coming.

After Jay and Diana got to their room and showered and changed Diana could not rest and wanted to go back. Jay took her back and when they got there Diana's mother told her that her grandfather wanted to see her and Jay. Diana ran to the room and Jay followed her. Diana's grandfather told her that she was the joy of his life and how proud of her he was. He told her that he always knew that she was a princess. Diana began to cry. Her grandfather then said, "Jay promise me that you'll always take care of her." He told Jay that he could see how much he loved Diana adding a love like yours will never die." Then he closed his eyes and died. It was as if he had waited for Diana and Jay to get there to die.

Diana screamed and cried. Jay took her out and told her that her grandfather had fought a long fight and that the battle was over and he was tired and now he was resting in peace. He held her and stroked her hair until they got to the car. They went home and Jay told Diana and her mother that he would pay for all the arrangements. The funeral was to be three days later.

The next day after her grandfather died Diana and Jay with some of her cousins went shopping in Lake Charles, where there was a large mall. Jay walked slowly, holding Diana's hand every step of the way and offering to buy her everything. Jay finally convinced Diana to but a navy blue dress to match the suit he was going to wear to the funeral.

Jay took Diana's cousins home and then he took Diana back to their room. Everyone knew how close Diana was to her grandfather and wanted to tell her how sorry they were. But Diana just wanted to be quiet and to her self. Jay entertained the visitors in the foyer while Diana rested in the bedroom. Diana's mother came over and went in the room where Diana was and they just held each other and cried. Jay heard his baby crying but he thought that he should just let her cry with her mother and get it all out. So he stayed where he was. It ended up the girls in the bedroom with Diana and the guys in the front room with Jay. Diana watched Them drink all night and the next day Diana's mother and her sister's made the Funeral arrangements. On the day of the funeral Diana was numb. She had Jay there to hold her and that made it easier for her.

After the funeral some of the relatives and friends all went back to the house and ate and drank until that night. When Jay and Diana got to the room they talked all night with Jay holding her. Diana told Jay that she wanted to leave in three days. For the next two days they visited everyone and thanked them, saying good-by. Jay told Diana that he wanted to spend some time with her alone, just the two of them. Diana said okay because her mother was going to stay two more weeks. Jay had given Diana's mother money and told her to stay as long as she wanted or needed to.

Jay told Diana that he wanted to spend time in New Orleans and do some sightseeing. Diana smiled and said okay. They arrived in New Orleans four hours later. Jay had his secretary reserve a room in the Marriott in downtown New Orleans in the middle of the French Quarters. They visited all the prominent areas in New Orleans and dined at the most famous places. They went in jazz clubs and had a good time. Diana almost forgot that she had just lost her grandfather. Jay wanted Diana to relax for a while and she did. Four days later they went home.

Jay's parents were so glad to see them that they did not let Diana out of their sight for hours. Jay's mother had made dinner and baked a cake. Diana thanked her and Jay's father and said that she loved them. Diana told Jay that she was going to get ready for and baked a cake. Diana thanked her and Jay's father and said that she loved them. Diana told Jay that she was going to get ready for work the next day. Jay told Diana to take some more time and rest. Diana told Jay that work would help her and that she had been gone long enough. Jay told Diana that he had enough money to take care of her and that he wished she didn't want to work. Diana told Jay that there were three things that were going to help her keep going, loving him, planning for their wedding, and her job. Jay held her and said, "I love the first two of them and I love you baby."

The next day when Diana got to work everyone was glad to see her and they welcomed her back. Diana bought so much joy everywhere she went. Jay came by to take Diana to lunch but she told him that she had too much to do. Jay ordered lunch in and they shared it while Diana kept working. Jay watched Diana work and knew that the company was on the rise with Diana in control of it.

THE WEDDING DAY

It was right after the Christmas holidays early in the new year and Diana was to be fitted for the second time for her wedding gown. She was excited. Also, Mrs. James, and Jay's mother were to be fitted for their dresses. Jay and his father were at home watching a ball game. The seamstress had almost finished Diana's dress and it fit perfectly. Diana was so pretty in the dress. The veil was finished and Diana was taking it home. The lady told Diana that her satin white Italian pumps were going to be made and flew in from Beverly Hills, California. She told Diana that the shoes cost two thousand dollars and that she would need a cashier's check. Diana agreed to bring the money by on Monday on their way home from work.

After the fitting they went out to lunch at the Red Lobster and talked about how beautiful Diana was going to be. When Diana got home and told Jay that she needed a cashiers check for two thousand dollars for her shoes Jay said, "What?" Jay never cared how much money Diana spent or what she bought but he had never heard of shoes being that much. Diana's mother stepped in and said, "Remember, Jay, these shoes are for a princess. "Jay looked at Diana and said "I think I'll send them ten thousand." Diana kissed him and said, "Baby, two thousand and not a penny more." Jay told Diana that he was going to go and order his father's and his suit's in March. Diana said "I love you baby." Jay said, "this really is happening, isn't it baby?" Diana told Jay that she was tired and she was going to lie down for a while. It was February 6, 1985 and what seemed like a peaceful night's rest turned into a nightmare. The phone rang and Jay's mother said "Jay, telephone." Jay was surprised because the only person who ever called him on his mother's phone was Diana and she was in the room asleep. When Jay got to the phone it was Diana's mother and Jay knew something was wrong. She said, "Jay, I have some bad news and I don't know if Diana can take this after her grandfather's death." She then told him Diana's father had just died and that they were bringing his body home for her to bury.

Jay said, "Oh no, not now! Please, not now." Diana's mother told Jay that she was on her way over and that she wanted to be there when Jay told Diana. Jay agreed and hung up. When Jay got off the phone and told his parents they also wanted to be there for Diana. They knew that the princess they all loved was going to be devastated. Jay went in the room where Diana was just lying quietly. He closed the door and Diana said "Baby, I'm not asleep. Come over here and show me how much you love me and lock the door." Jay said "Baby I love you more than anything in this world." Diana sensed something was wrong. "Jay what is wrong? Are your parents alright?" Jay said "Yes." Diana's mother walked in, and Diana got up and said "What is wrong?" Jay walked over and said "Baby, sit down." Diana said, "I don't want to sit down! What is wrong." Jay put his arms around her and held her and said, "Baby your father just had a heart attack and died." Diana started to scream and cry and say "God, please help me now!" She fell to her knees and her mother held her and said, "I'm sorry, Baby." They all sat in Jay's room and talked all night. Diana said, "Jay, I was just thinking and I don't know if I could marry you now. I can't even be given away by my father." Jay said, "Baby, that's not a problem, and we can talk about that later."

Diana's family came up from Louisiana for the funeral and she met aunt's on her father's side that she never knew. After the funeral a few family members came by Diana's mother house and they ate and drank all night.

The next day Diana went back to work and continued working for the next two weeks. Jay kept in close touch with Diana because she was taking this too well and he was scared for her. One day Diana was at work and she was thinking of her father and started to cry so she called Jay to take her home. He took her down to Haynes Point Park and they walked and talked all day. Diana cried, talked, and prayed as Jay listened. When they got home Diana told Jay that she had to go home. Jay said, "Dee you are home." Diana said, "Baby, I mean home to my house." She told him, "We are going to be married in three months and I can't be living with you. That is not how I dreamed we would start. Jay argued, "You don't live here you just sleep here. You have not changed your address yet." Diana replied, "Baby please try to understand that I have to go home for three months. I love you so much and it's going to be hard not sleeping with you but we both have to try." Jay said, "I love you so much." Diana said, "I'm counting on it." Jay kissed her and Diana packed to leave.

When Jay took Diana home he stayed until late that night as he would do every night until they got married.

The day had come for Diana to pick up and try on her dress for the final time. Diana's dress and shoes were so beautiful that even she did not expect that she could look so pretty. Diana truly was going to be the prettiest bride ever married.

When Diana bought her dress to Jay's house. She made him promise not to look at it. While Diana was placing her dress and shoes away, Jay and his parents were talking about who would give her away. Jay's father listened in on different ideas, then shared his own. "Son I have loved you all my life. I watched you grow into the man I dreamed you would be. Then you bought Diana into our lives and if ever a child had paid their parents back for bringing

97

them into this world you did by giving us this gift. I was the happiest man alive when I heard the news of you two getting married. I love you both so much. If I had made Diana myself I couldn't have loved her more. She truly is a wonderful person. I waited all my life to stand by you when you got married and even when you were four I pictured us side by side at your wedding. It's every father's joy. But son I think Diana needs me more, so I would like to give Diana away. It will be double joy to walk by daughter down the isle and give her to my son. How many fathers can say they have had that joy." Jay's mother stood up and kissed her husband and said, "I don't think I have ever loved you more than for what you just shared with us" Jay stood up, moved to tears. He said, "Dad, thank you. I will always love you."

Then Diana walked in and everyone was in tears and hugging. She said "I should be the one crying and nervous. I am the bride." Jay smiled and reached for Diana and kissed her. He told her to sit down for a minute. "I just want to look at you for a few precious moments." Diana said, "Jay please don't start about me going home tonight." He said, "Baby anything you want anyway you want it is yours." Diana looking surprised said, "Really! Well I would like to have my baby marry me." Jay answered, "It will be done." Jay's father said, "Diana, my daughter, I love you and I would be honored if you let me give you away." Diana was surprised again, and answered "Thank you but Jay needs you and I could not ask him to give me you on that day." Jay said, Diana I gave my parents to you a long time ago and it's what I want." Diana got up and walked over to Jay's father and said, You have been the only father I've known in a long time and I love you. I would be honored if you gave me away. Thank you." Diana started to cry and then Jay said, "Let's celebrate over some champagne." His mother said, "I was saving this for after the wedding but we can get some more if we need it. Diana and Jay spent the night together, making love all night.

Two weeks later was a rehearsal day. Jay had asked his best friend Marvin to be his best man and Diana's maid of honor was her favorite cousin Mel. Mel and Marvin had been intimate friends before but they were just friends now, The church was the New Macedonian Baptist Church on Minnesota and Alabama Avenue's S.E. The preacher was Rev. Cobert Hall. Jay and Marvin had been hanging out and were late for rehearsal. When Jay walked in Diana was upset. "Jay , we need to do this right. Please take it more seriously." She was wearing a white dress with white pumps and looked beautiful. When Jay noticed how good she looked he said "Baby you look good enough to marry now." Diana said, "Please Jay." He said, "Baby could I kiss you," and put his arms around Diana. Diana said, " Jay after you kiss me can we start this rehearsal. Jokingly he said, "How about we go in the back for a while then come back and start this," Diana moved to walk away and Jay said, "Okay I'll settle for a kiss." He kissed Diana and showed her he wanted more. They started the rehearsal and everything went well.

Jay took the wedding party to dinner at Houston's in Rockville afterwards and thanked them all. Diana gave all the girls gold bracelet for waiting on her and the guys gold tie pins. That night when Jay took Diana home he asked her to come back home with him. Diana said no and said that they had only seven days before they would be married and she had to stay at home until then. Jay said okay. Diana was surprised that Jay said okay so quickly. She didn't realize that Jay had planned to stay with her at her house all night. About two AM that morning Diana asked Jay to go home and go to bed. Jay agreed and promised to be back in a couple of hours.

The next day Jay was back at Diana's house and they spent a quiet evening in Diana's room talking about their future together. On the Tuesday before the wedding Jay told Diana that on Friday night, the guys were giving him a bachelor's party. Diana told Jay that she wished he would not go. Jay said, "Baby it's just a party for fun." Diana said, "A party with women and alcohol. I want you to be fresh and feeling well on Saturday when we get married." Jay said that he would not stay long. On that Friday Diana asked Jay not to go and to come to her house and stay with her. Jay also knew that Diana was trying to keep him from the party. He also knew that the party would wait for him. So Jay went over and stayed with Diana until she fell asleep about eleven PM. Diana kissed Jay good night and asked him to go home. Jay said okay and left. Jay went straight to the party and everyone was glad to see him. They partied hard and long. About three AM Jay realized that he missed Diana. He said good night to all the people at the party and said that he had to go. Jay drove straight back to Diana's house. He sat on her porch until daylight.

At about six AM Jay yelled for Diana and she heard him. Diana said, "Jay what are you doing here? If you see me I will have to cancel the wedding." Jay said, "Baby I have been here since three o'clock. I had to be near you. I love you so much and I wanted to tell you." Diana said, "Jay, I needed to hear that this morning. Thank you. Now honey go home and get some rest so you can get dressed and be on time to marry me." Jay said "Nothing in life can keep me away."

Jay went home and Diana got up and ate breakfast. Her mother and aunts were up early and waiting to help Diana. The wedding was at twelve o'clock and it was ten when Diana took her shower and started to getting ready. Jay's mother called and told Diana that she would be at the church to wait on her. Diana thanked her and told her that she loved her very much. Diana was all dressed and ready to go. Jay had a white limo waiting for Diana and her mother and maid of honor. They arrived at the church twenty minutes late.

The news media was out front waiting to talk to Diana about her marriage. Diana couldn't understand why they would be interested in a small-time wedding. Diana did not know yet that she was marrying a millionaire. Reporters followed Diana to the church.

Diana was dressed so beautifully the whole church was astonished. When she walked to the front of the church Jay's father went to meet her, she was the prettiest girl in the world. As she walked up to Jay and he said, "I think I'm going to faint. I had no idea you could ever be any more beautiful. You are breathtaking." Jay reached for Diana's waist and held her. The preacher waved for Jay to get back in place but he did not move. He never stopped looking at Diana as if he were going to kiss her. Jay's father said, "Son, we should get started now." But Jay still never moved. The church started talking and the preacher said, "Jay, lets get started." Diana looked at Jay and said, "Baby I have waited for a long time for this day. Please don't kiss me. The service will be over in twenty minutes and I don't want you to ever stop kissing me. Please baby." Jay took Diana's hand and stepped in place for the ceremony.

The preacher began by saying that he had never seen a more beautiful bride. He compared Diana to a princess. Jay never let Diana's hand go until it was time to place the ring on her finger. After the wedding vows Jay kissed Diana so long that his father had to stop him. As they walked out the church he never let Diana go. When she threw her bouquet Jay's hands were around her waist. After Diana and Jay got to LaFontaine Bleu in New Carrolton, Maryland for the reception it was time for Diana to take her garter off and Jay raised her dress and removed the delicate pink and white band. He then acted as if he was going to throw it and then put it in his pocket. The guys fussed and teased Jay as they were

101

celebrating. When Diana and Jay got ready to leave the party was just starting to go strong. They had a nine o'clock flight to catch which gave them enough time to change and get to the airport. Diana did not know where Jay was taking her. He just told her to pack very little. Diana had one suitcase and Jay had three. They were going to start their honeymoon with two weeks in Hawaii and ended with two weeks in Paris.

While in Hawaii Jay had a designer bring Diana a wardrobe to choose from for her stay in the islands. He did the same thing when they got to Paris. Diana now knew why he told her to pack very little. Diana and Jay spent three weeks making love and being together alone. They were both very much in love.

When it was time to go home Jay told Diana that their life was just beginning and that he would make her the happiest wife ever married. Diana said that she was already the happiest wife in the world, and that she loved him.

A DREAM COME TRUE

It was a Monday night when Diana and Jay got home to Jay's parent's house. His parents were glad to see them. They hugged and kissed them with joy. After dinner Diana and Jay went to their room and got in bed. Jay and Diana were newlyweds, so they did very little sleeping that night. The next day Jay told Diana that he wanted to give her a wedding gift. Diana said that he didn't have to buy her anything else and that he had given her enough. Diana said, "Baby we are going to have the rest of our lives to buy gifts. I don't need a gift now." Jay said, trust me. We want this gift." Diana said, "Okay, but I have to go home when we have finished." Jay said, "Baby we are married and your home is with me now." Diana said, "I know, I mean I have to get the rest of my things." Jay agreed. Jay took Diana to Suitland Road, S.E., two houses down from where the mayor of the city lived and he parked his car. He got out and went around the car to open Diana's door. Diana was puzzled and asked "Jay why are we here?" He replied, "follow me and trust me." Diana smiled and said okay.

They walked up some stairs and on to the porch of the house and opened the door. The house had three bedrooms up stairs and one downstairs. The large master bedroom had a bathroom, just as spacious, with the bath tub separate from the shower. The bathtub was the size of a small swimming pool. The shower was the size of a small room. The closet was large with rotating poles going up and down around. Diana could easily fill the closet with all the clothes Jay bought her and would buy her. The kitchen was large and constructed almost entirely of marble. The living room was huge with a large fireplace. Another fireplace was in the bedroom. The downstairs bathroom was large also. The house was gorgeous and Diana was speechless.

103

Jay said, "Baby welcome to our new home." Diana said, "Baby I love you so much, Thank you. When we have kids there will be plenty of space for them." Jay said, Diana, let's make love in our new house." Diana said, "Baby, please. Let's go buy furniture and drapes and pots and pans and dishes and towels to fix our new home up so we can move in by Friday." Jay said, "Diana, we have the rest of our lives." Diana said, "Baby I want our first time in here to be special. I want a candlelight dinner cooked by me and a cake that I baked and a fire in our room with champagne. I really want this to be a special time for us. One that we will share for the rest of our lives." Jay made a call to his office and had his secretary send over the top three designers in the area to decorate their new house.

Jay and Diana went to buy furniture. The living room set was white with marble end tables. The bedroom was cherry wood with a very tall chest. The dinning room was cherry wood also. When they got back home the designers were there waiting for them. Diana picked light peach drapes for the living room with matching accessories. The bedroom was all red and white fit for a queen. They had the room downstairs in mint green and one room upstairs in pale yellow. The other rooms upstairs was in pink. Their furniture was to be delivered on Thursday and the designers were to be finished by Saturday, and Diana and Jay planned to move in on Monday. Finally the house was decorated. Jay had Diana's clothes moved in and put in place in her rotating closet on Saturday. He had her shoes put in the same order as the clothes she matched them with. Diana was so pleased.

On Monday morning Diana got up and woke Jay up; she was excited about moving in their new house. Diana told jay that they had to go to the grocery store so that she could cook dinner for their special night. Jay got up and dressed and they went to the store. Their bill was two hundred dollars. They bought enough food for a family of ten. Diana went home and cooked. She cooked shrimp stuffed with crab meat and cabbage and potatoes with a lemon cake. Jay lit the candles and they sat down to eat. Diana and Jay took one bite of the food and jay kissed Diana and they were on the floor kissing. They made love in the living room and then they went upstairs, where Jay had a fire lit and a bottle of champagne on ice with two glasses by the bed. They drank and made love in front of the fireplace. Before they knew it the sun was up so they went to sleep.

At twelve o'clock Diana woke up and saw that Jay was already up. He had cleaned the kitchen and put all the food away. Jay told Diana that he had his office screen some housekeepers for them to interview today. Diana said, "Jay I can be the housekeeper." Jay said, "Baby, this is a big house and I want you here for me not to clean this house." Diana said, "Jay, I could have done both." Jay told Diana to please consider having a housekeeper. Diana told Jay that she didn't want a housekeeper. Jay told her that they needed a housekeeper even if she was just there five days a week. Diana finally agreed to interview the housekeepers. They interviewed seven ladies from ages thirty-five to fifty-five. They picked Emma, a lady who had been housekeeping thirty years and had just lost her husband and just wanted to take care of somebody. The old lady fell in love with Jay right away. Diana liked her honesty. She asked her to work from Monday to Friday and Jay offered to pay her thirty thousand dollars a year. Emma agreed. She was probably the highest paid house keeper in the area. Her check was made up as if she worked for Jay at his company. Jay went back to work after four weeks in their new home.

One Thursday when Jay came home, Diana told him that she wanted to have their parents over for dinner on Friday. Diana told him she had asked Emma to cook a meal for six. Jay agreed. He asked Diana what could he do? Diana said, Baby I just need you to love me." Jay picked Diana up and carried her upstairs to the bedroom where they made love through the night.

The next day Diana and Jay entertained and the dinner went well. Diana was telling her mother that she was going back to work next week and that she wanted her to look for a better place to live. Diana told her that she wanted to buy her a condominium on the top of Pennsylvania Avenue, Maryland. She told her that it was a nice neighborhood and that she would feel more safe there. Diana told her that the condo was large and not too far from her. Diana's mother agreed, but told her that she was going to borrow some money from Jay to buy a new car because the one she had was dead. Diana said, Mother, I will buy you a new car too. Mrs. James hugged her daughter and said, "Baby you really are a princess. If I only did one thing right in life it was you." Diana said, "Mother, I love you for it." Diana and her mother were hugging when the others came into the kitchen and they all watched. Jay said "Baby, dinner was great and I love you." The guest went into the living room to watch television and Diana told Jay she would tell him what she and her mother was talking about later. Jay agreed, and they went into the living room.

After their parents left, Jay and Diana went upstairs to the bedroom and Diana started telling Jay she was going back to work the following week. Jay said, "Is that what you and your mother were talking about? Diana I'm not ready for you to go back to work yet." Diana told him that he would never be ready because he didn't want her to work. She said, "baby I have to work. I have to be responsible and needed." Jay said, "Baby I need you. I need you here at home." Diana said, "I will be here when you are here baby. Please let me go back to work now. I have to buy my mother a condo that I looked at before I left and she needs a new car." Jay said, "We can buy that with my job." Diana said, "Jay I am going to work Monday." Jay told Diana that he wanted to have a baby or two before she went back to work. Diana said, "Working women have babies all the time." Jay said, "Baby please don't go." Diana said, "Jay I have to." Jay went downstairs in disgust. Diana showered and went to bed.

Two hours passed and Jay had still not come upstairs so Diana went downstairs to get him. He was watching TV. Diana called out to him "I miss you baby. Please come to bed." She then went over and kissed him, saying that she loved him. Jay said "I love you too baby." Diana asked Jay if they could go and see the condo tomorrow and buy her mother a Volvo. Jay said, "Yes." Diana held her hand out and Jay reached for it and Diana led him to the steps, cutting off lights behind her. Jay picked Diana up and carried her into their room and put her on the bed and they made love to each other.

The next day Jay and Diana went to look at the condo and Jay purchased it as a business investment. They then went to the Volvo dealer and purchased a white Volvo and drove it to Diana's mother apartment. They told her to start packing so that she could move in to her new condo in two weeks. Diana told her mother that they would decorate the condo together at Diana's expense. Mrs. James was so happy that she kissed Jay and Diana both at the same time.

Diana had gotten out of the ghetto and took her mother out with her. Even as a little girl Diana used to dream that someday she and her mother would live in a middle-class neighborhood. They would not live together, but they were living much better.

Diana went back to work and was living a happy life. Then one day Terry Bradly came into Diana's office and told her that she

107

was going to stay in charge of Diana's office because she had been gone too long. Diana called the manager in and he told Terry that Diana would be back in charge. Terry said, "I should have known that after all you are sleeping with the owner." Diana said, "What did you say?" Terry said "You heard me. I have heard of sleeping with the boss but marrying him. That's a little extreme isn't it? " Diana looked up and asked the manager who owned the company and he said he had to go and would be back to discuss it later. Diana grabbed her purse and went over to Jay's office building, which was just six blocks down. When she got there Jay was in a meeting. Diana walked in and told Jay that she wanted to speak to him now. Jay could see that Diana was upset. He said, "My boss has spoken. Continue on and I will join you if I can, if not, Bennett will handle it. " Jay walked over to his office where Diana was. By this time Diana had figured most of the puzzle out. She remembered how Jay would always talk to the boss about her leaving and her time off. He was the boss all the time! Why didn't he tell me? She was crying.

Jay walked in and said, "Baby what's wrong?" Diana said, "I thought we were happy, I thought you loved me. I thought as husband and wife we shared everything." Jay said, "We do and don't ever doubt my love for you." Diana said, "You love me enough to own the company I work for and not tell me. I have to hear it from someone else." Diana told him what Terry said and he reached for her to hold her. Diana asked Jay how could he do that to her? Jay said, "Diana I wanted to marry you more than anything in this world. I would have bought a country to marry you, I love you so much. Diana, when you said you had to have a job before you married me and you would not work for me I was desperate. It started out as me being a board member. Then when Terry started giving you problems I wanted to ease your pain., so I bought the company. I was going to tell you that night you told me you were going back to work and when I started you touched me and we started making love. I took it off my mind and then it didn't seem to matter." Diana said, Jay, we are a team. We decide together what matters and what doesn't." Jay said, "Remember when I told you that you are my boss. Those words are so true. You see if I hadn't fallen in love with you that day you walked into my house I would still be selling drugs on the streets. I would not have any of the things we have today. I owe this all to you. This is all ours and if I were to die today or tomorrow it is all yours. Please believe that I love you more than anything in this world." Diana said, "Let's go home baby. Jay said, "Please understand that I did it for us. I live and breath for you." After talking Jay took Diana home.

The next day they spent all day talking and playing, and on Sunday they went to church and then went to Jay's parent's house for dinner. On Monday Jay called a board meeting at the company where Diana worked. At the meeting Jay gave Diana the company and all of his shares. Diana was stunned. She immediately took charge. She fired Terry and put her secretary in charge. Terry walked out and slammed the door. Diana made some more changes and left to spend the day with her husband.

They went to the park and walked along the water all day. Then they went home and talked the rest of the night. Diana and Jay lived happily ever after. Their love was like a fairy tale. Their lives were a dream come true.

About The Author

My name is ada Sherrill, I was born at Walter Reed Army Medical Hospital, in Washington, D.C., on August 19, 1959. My Mother Elouise (James) Sherrill, (now Temoney) was born in New Orleans, Louisiana. My father Willie E. Sherrill was born in Memphis, Tennessee.

I have two older sisters, Darlene (Sherrill) Harris and Katherine A. Sherrill. My brother was born seven years after me. My mother met and later married his father Robert L. Temoney. My step father has been like a father to me since he has been in my life. When my father came back into my life after I was older he became my biological father and my step father continued to be the father figure in my life.

My brother Darrien Temoney (T-Bone) was brutally murdered on December 6, 1987 in S.E. Washington, D.C. He was shot in the head five times and left to die on the street. It was my faith in God that gave me the strength to go on. My family and I are very close and it was this closeness that helped us through this most tragic period in our lives.

In the past I have said and heard others say "It (the pain) will get better with time," before Darrien's murder I never truly understood the meaning of that statement. Seven years later the pain has decreased, with time. I thank God everyday for being with me through that. Now at thirty-five, married with two children; I am better able to stay focused on the healing process and go on with my life.

I have learned to "Let Go and Let GOD."

I think High School was the most memorable part of my life. It was there that I learned to open up and share important parts of my life to include some of my inner most personal feelings. One of the better friends I met while still in high school was the man I eventually married, Bobby Mills, eleven years older, a consummate lecturer, and the most instrumental person other than my mother, I can think of who helped me adjust and be best prepared for my adult life.

My aim for personal achievement is high, I consider owning my business and obtaining financial security while doing so a means for measuring my success. I would like to accept that challenge because, for most of my younger years it was made clear to me that people like me were not able to obtain any type of business success and that I should only prepare myself for public assistance, public service, prison, or death as my only avenues for life.

As a result of those type of lessons, it has taken me to this point to seek methods for overcoming the very extensive comprehensive brain washing I received as an African American female. Even while preparing this book, I called where I once lived (public housing) a ghetto. It was when I found the wherewithal to look the word up, did I realize that it was a slur against minorities in general and African Americans in particular.

I've now come to the realization that there are many self improvement methods I must seek in order to be the complete person I am seeking. I now am using all of the lessons available through the most wonderful teacher other than GOD the almighty, life.

During life 101, I am able to see more clearly a better way of living. I am now challenged with living in that manner, hoping that my illustrations will be a format for others to follow.

My memoirs includes the readings of positive speakers and authors, mostly of the African American race and specifically African American females-for whom else is better qualified to share similar experiences; a complete commitment to my faith in GOD THE FATHER, for where else can I turn when all else fails; my mother and sisters-for when no other human being is willing to help, close family members will; my husband of many years-for no other man can be a better man to me than him; my children- for through them I see hope and a need for me to do my very best at contributing to making this a better world to live in; friends - for through them I have discovered more about myself; the oppressors of the world - for through them I found a cause and until there are no more oppressors, I have a purpose in life!

How does owning a business and being financially secure demonstrate and determine my degree of success? While learning about the history of African American people, I learned that there were a great many oppressors, and they put forth a concerted effort in ensuring that the level of education for African Americans was kept low. They put together very elaborate schemes to ensure that African Americans weren't successful in business without one of them being in control of that business and ultimately gaining the largest profit or even eliminating that African American altogether as the business demonstrated a potential for high earnings.

I learned that African Americans are mentioned briefly in the lessons of American History. The ones who appear to receive recognition by other than African American historical scholars are those who best served on the behalf of the oppressors or their points. It is my aim to establish success so that history can be written about another African American who achieved admirably without being the subject of others. I intend to be a role model if for no others, then for my children. Not to say that success is measured in financial worth or social status. To be able to offer others something I possess is the ultimate example I can demonstrate. I can offer self worth, pride and goals for achievement; regardless of what your beginnings are. I can offer ideas and demonstrate how easy it can be to be cohabitants on this planet, peacefully. I can offer a smile and friendliness to a sad and friendless person. I can offer kindness and gentleness even to one who choose to be my enemy.

So, I would like for it to be written, that I made a positive impact on this planet and specifically with African Americans.

My intermediate goal is to run my own publishing company with a magazine I will name "Foresight", which will be intended for holding politicians accountable for what they said to get elected. I have always had an interest in politics and what may drive people to it.

I have studied local African American politicians. During my studies I have either read quotes or heard most if not all of the politicians of my research make the campaign promises which went unfilled after achieving office. I would like to be a constant reminder to the voters of the promises that their elected officials made and give those very same officials an opportunity to respond to the concerns of their constituency during their political tenure.

I met with Earl Graves and John Johnson, Publishers of Black Enterprise and Ebony/ Jet Magazines, while attending a Networking Conference in Chicago, at the River Front Sheraton, in 1993. I learned a lot about the magazine business and was exposed to many of the ideas and methods of being successful in the publishing industry. I will be able to draw on this experience while setting up my business.

I will continue to work hard to make a difference for you and me!